COMPLETELY UNDATABLE

A FRIENDS TO LOVERS ROMANTIC COMEDY

BRITTNI MINER

EBURNEAN
BOOKS

COMPLETELY
UNDATABLE

For Steve: Thanks for making bad jokes at weddings, eating way too much food with me, and always making me smile.

KEEP IN TOUCH

Enjoy Brittni's writing? Join her readers group to be the first to know about upcoming releases, beta reading opportunities, deals, and more.

Join the Brittni Miner Readers Group

CHAPTER 1

SUMMER

Viola Reed was stuck. For the life of her, she could not figure out how to get Jean-Luc to take his shirt off.

He's sweating, maybe? It had been done too many times. *It's pouring down rain?* Nope, that was *The Notebook*. *It's cold and his warm shirt is needed elsewhere?* No, no. He'd get cold himself. The reason had to be believable; otherwise, the story just wouldn't work.

Viola paused, chewing on her nails as she thought.

Aha! Something spills on him. That would do the trick. It had worked once in *Midnight Magic*, but no one read her stuff back then anyway. Readers wouldn't remember the plot device now.

She began to type up the scene, relishing the satisfying *click-clack* of her keyboard. Finally, she was hitting her groove.

Viola took a lot of pride in her work as a romance novelist. It wasn't that she particularly liked what she was writing about. In fact, it was quite the opposite; she thought that the genre had grown tired and stale. After all, how many rainy kissing scenes and characters with billowing blouses and heaving bosoms did one actually see in the real world?

Viola believed in the idea of romance, and she maybe (sometimes) even wished that all those kissing scenes popped up a bit more in reality. Unfortunately, to her, life simply fell short of what was written on the page. Or rather, life fell short of what was written on every single page of every single romance being published these days. The genre had grown tired.

Truth be told, Viola had become a grade A cynic, tried and tested. But it was her skepticism that made her excel at her craft. She'd discovered early on in her career that she could pump out novel after novel, prioritize quantity over quality by cashing in on all the worn-out tropes.

Sometimes her method made her write a bit like a zombie, churning out the same goods over and over again without really having to use her brain. But every now and then, she was lucky enough to stumble on a truly complex story, something that called out the clichés for what they were. And reaching the end of one of those stories—reaching that satisfying feeling of trapping the tropes in pen and paper—helped her to feel like she could skewer the falsehoods, banish them from her own life, and make a pretty penny doing it.

And people *ate* it up! Viola got emails every day from devoted readers, and sometimes even actual paper letters. She liked to read them the same way that other people liked to relax with TV or social media. After a long day, she'd curl up on her couch wearing a robe and slippers, let her tabby cat, Duncan, cuddle between her knees, and review her stack of mail.

She knew that many of these women (okay, maybe *all* of these women) weren't as cynical as she was. They believed that the kissing in the rain really happened, that her latest version of Fabio was always hanging around to save the day. She would smile at the praise she'd get, laugh at the funny stories from love-struck teens, and scoff at those that took her material a little too seriously.

But all the while, she knew there was some small part of her that envied her more optimistic and idealistic readers. It was something that pushed her to keep checking the letters every day because reading about the hope that these women had in the world, about the hope they had in love, helped her to feel less empty inside. Less depressed that her characters were fiction and not fact.

Viola kept the mail bound and organized in her desk drawer, always ready for a quick read. She kept her favorites in a little stack in the front, so she could easily reread them during a writing slump. Save for her extra pens and pads and her prized antique collection of Walt Whitman poems, the letters were the only things she bothered to keep around for inspirational purposes. Maybe she *herself* was a cliché. Ugh.

But Jean-Luc and his stupid shirt had been a hurdle for her. It felt good to finally have the climax of her newest novel behind her.

How long had it been since sunrise? The light was streaming in through the bay window where Viola's desk looked out, lighting up the jagged Atlanta skyline in brilliant shades of pink and orange. The world looked like it had only just woken up with the sun's rays. The tiny green fern on her balcony still dripped delicate beads of dew, and her sleepy neighbors were beginning to peek their heads out of their apartment windows to breathe in the last vestige of clean city air before traffic pollution kicked in.

Atlanta was its own beast, a far cry from the likes of

either New York or L.A. It was driven by an interesting dichotomy: big business and soul food. It was a combination which usually manifested in high-profile suits walking by Viola's window, forking barbecue out of a Styrofoam container while they took a lunchtime call. Sunrise was a welcome respite from it all, Viola's uncontested favorite time of day in which the corporations were still asleep, but the smell of grits and eggs floated through the air as the soul food joints started up their stovetops.

Viola got up from her desk at the window, stretching her arms up over her head and feeling the satisfying pop of her uncurled toes. She bent forward, letting her long, black hair sweep over her face as she curved her back. She'd been up writing all through the night, and her body was paying the price. Duncan's small orange face popped between her legs, appearing before her as upside down. He meowed loudly, eyes darting to the snack cupboard behind them.

"Yeah, yeah," Viola said, laughing and reaching to retrieve the orange furball. "I was just finishing up."

She hugged him close, ignoring his desperate struggle to jump from her arms and lead her to the snacks. Viola placed him on the counter as she found his can of food and dumped some into his food bowl. She brought the bowl over to him, dumping a little extra in before passing it on. He jumped in ferociously, all pretense of affection for Viola abandoned when food was on the line. She couldn't help but smile. *Spoiled baby.*

Her glass of wine from the late-night writing marathon still sat next to the stovetop. Viola picked it up and sniffed at it, wondering if it would still taste okay after breathing for such a long time. After a moment's consideration, she decided to risk it, throwing back the rest of the glass despite the "a.m." digits clearly displayed on her alarm clock.

She'd been drinking a lot lately. Too much, probably. She'd been playing it a little fast and loose, trying to keep up with her writing calendar and her limited social life. *Any* social life at all felt like running a marathon for the introverted Viola, and recently a little pick-up in her extra-curriculars had her feeling exhausted and even more cynical than usual. She was right in the thick of the worst time of year for a romantic skeptic: the dreaded wedding season.

Viola had known this time of life would be coming, but a little foresight didn't make things any less bearable. Such was the consequence of having been a part of a deeply Southern sorority back in college: the women she'd surrounded herself with had been the kind that were still expected to get married young and pop out babies right away, courtesy of overbearing mothers with monogrammed purses and daddies who threatened every date they brought home with a shotgun hung on the living room wall. While Viola herself had managed to escape the power of the ring, the swift approach of age thirty had brought the first onslaught of engagements announced on Facebook and Instagram. Because God forbid any social debutant end up a spinster in the 21st century. *Bless her little sad heart.*

The courtesy invitations from her sorority sisters had started coming in the early winter months and kept arriving in a steady stream until the spring. Viola had decided to keep out two or three of them, tucked away for a quick reference when she needed character inspiration or when she crafted a mood board for her newest saccharine-sweet plot outline.

But the attempt at using her real life to inspire her fiction was hitting a little too close to home. These were her friends, her sorority sisters getting married, and the personal nature of it all unnerved her. She hadn't once pulled the invitations out of their drawer to look at them since she'd put them away in the first place.

She'd known the two most special invitations were coming before she received them, of course, and known that she wouldn't be able to squirrel them away out of sight like the rest. Still, seeing them tacked onto her refrigerator had made it feel too real. Knowing that her best friend and her sister would both be getting married this year meant that Viola was in for more late nights spent in uncomfortable heels, away from the safety of her laptop's glow, and being harassed by some handsy groomsmen.

Attending a long list of wedding receptions made Viola feel like eligible bachelors were the hunters and she was the nerdy, old maid deer. Where were the camo and guns for this type of season? They seemed only natural extensions for the hungry single men of Atlanta. Viola licked the rim of her glass clean as she was lost in disturbing thought about her future on the hunting grounds of a wedding.

Back on the little desk, her phone vibrated. She crossed the room, picking it up to check the caller ID. *RUBY*. She clicked the tiny green key, balancing the phone on her shoulder as she started to clean up the chaos that was her micro apartment during the work week.

"Roo! Hey!" It took a little effort for Violet to inject cheer into her voice this early in the morning after a sleepless night.

"I didn't wake you up, right?" The soft, lilting voice of her stepsister made Viola smile. Ruby was younger by a few years, but always the more precocious, mature one. She checked in on Viola every week, sometimes every day, despite her busy job in advertising.

"No, no. I've been burning the midnight oil on my latest sequel," Viola said, popping open the fridge to check for some semblance of breakfast. A sad array of expired products and half-eaten sandwiches stared back at her.

"I wish you'd take it easy," Ruby fretted.

Viola smiled. Her sister, like all others, constantly worried about Viola's bohemian, "creative" lifestyle as a professional writer. And their worries weren't entirely unfounded. Viola was knocking at thirty's door and yet she lived alone (Ruby didn't count Duncan) in the middle of busy, bustling Atlanta. She survived on takeout from the Chinese restaurant down the street. And, admittedly, the hours she kept were a little weird depending on if she had a good Netflix series to binge all day into the night. She had no patience for a roommate, so she forked over most of her writing money to live in her slightly above-average apartment alone and in peace.

But she could write whenever, wherever, and however she wanted! It was absolute perfection. Having a flexible schedule and a preference for alone-time didn't make her any less emotionally mature than her sorority sisters with the nine-to-five gigs and the shiny engagement rings. No one else needed to understand.

"I've got things under control, captain." Viola pulled a Tupperware of leftover breakfast casserole from the fridge and hip-bumped the appliance shut behind her. She scooped up a piece with her bare fingers and popped it into her mouth, immediately gagging at the sour taste of food gone bad. She wallowed in silence, hoping that Ruby wouldn't make out the irony.

"I was just calling to make sure you got the dress I sent over," Ruby said. "You *did* remember that Hannah's rehearsal dinner is tonight, right?"

Viola could hear the worry in her voice, and she could picture her sister now, tucked into the armchair in her front room as she always was after work before Scott got home. She would be nervously twisting a strand of long blonde hair as she pursed her pink, heart-shaped lips and fretted over her haphazard older sibling. Viola's mother had left when she was little, and Ruby and her own attentive, scrupulous mother Andrea had stepped right in and taken her place. Up until Andrea lost her battle with cancer just two years prior, Viola had all the mothering anyone would ever need. And then some.

Still... even watchful family members couldn't help her sense of organization. Viola spotted the green dress still hanging in its plastic bag by her front door where Scott had dropped it off for her last week. The rehearsal dinner. *Shoot!*

"Ready to go!" Viola promised, scooping the dress of its hanger and quietly removing the plastic to hold it up to her body. She dashed to the hall mirror, sizing herself up.

"If it needs dry cleaning, I can take it over for a rush job."

"Come on; have a little faith in me," Viola lied, turning to the side to see how it might fit on her body. "I've had it all taken care of for days."

The dress had certainly become a little worse for wear in its crumpled bag, but Viola was not about to admit that to her sister. It was a beautiful color, sea green in the perfect shade for her tanned complexion. The dress even brought out the hazel flecks in her dark eyes.

Viola was a quarter Native American on her father's side, a fact that she largely forgot about until she glanced in the mirror and saw the vaguest resemblance to the rapper Princess Nokia. The writer inside of her insisted that she not reduce herself down to some stereotype or anything, but Viola couldn't help but think that she looked a bit like an off-brand version of Disney's Pocahontas. She pulled her thick black hair back, knotting it at the top of her head and turning to admire the jutting, prominent lines of her jaw and cheekbones. She could definitely work with this.

"Scott and I will pick you up, but remember to bring along your toast. Hannah will *freak* if you improv the way you did at her bachelorette party." It wasn't meant as a stab, rather a jest. Viola could hear the smile in Ruby's voice.

Viola headed back toward her bedroom, the dress slung across one arm as she carefully stepped over Duncan, who had returned to beg for more snacks. She spread the soft silk out on her comforter, eyeballing the room as she tried to remember where she'd last stashed her iron.

"I've got the toast," Viola assured her. "If there's one thing I'm good for, it's a bit of writing. And there's always been plenty to say about Han. I'll keep the jokes about her teenage back brace and Nick Jonas obsession to a minimum."

"I'm sure she'll appreciate that," Ruby laughed. "You're going to make a great Maid of Honor."

"No promises," Viola said, smirking. She plucked the iron from its obscure spot behind a mound of unfolded laundry. Could one actually iron silk? She hesitated, hovering with the plug next to the wall. She thought better of it and snatched up the dress, heading to the bathroom to get the shower nice and steamy instead.

"Which reminds me..." Ruby started. Her voice was halting, hesitant.

Viola stopped in her tracks, picking the phone up off her shoulder. "Roo? You ok?"

"Of course," Ruby laughing, the soft, tinkling sound instantly relaxing Viola. "It's just—well, I feel sort of silly asking. You're my sister, after all. But with Scott and I getting married in May and now you'll have had a little practice in the spotlight—"

"Spit it out," Viola admonished, one hand on her hip. Sometimes Ruby could start rambling when she wanted to ask for something, and she wouldn't stop unless someone pushed her to.

"Would you be my Maid of Honor, too? You wouldn't have to do much, I promise. I like to have control, we all know that. I'll make my own plans and call my own venues, so you'll only have to—"

"Of course I will, Roo." A soft small tugged up the corners of Viola's mouth. "I'd be honored."

And she meant it, too. Through everything important in her life, her sister had been there. They had held hands together in the playroom when Viola's father would come home smelling of another woman's perfume, making Andrea cry. Ruby had been the first one to read Viola's earliest short stories; she'd laughed in the right places and given the most insightful notes. And in the tenth grade, when Viola's mother gave up her weeks with Vi to move across the country and start a new family with a handsome husband and perfect, blonde children... Ruby had been there then, too. And she had been the one that reminded her that the most important family was the one you chose for yourself.

Above all, though, Vi's favorite memories with Ruby were of reading from her Whitman collection together. The little leather-bound book of poems had gotten worn out and faded over the years from where the girls had read them together. They would steal away after bedtime and use flashlights under their comforters, reading. They'd quote at each other when boys broke their hearts back in grade school.

The book was the one thing that Viola could remember having gotten from her mother. It was a throwaway gift, something her mom had found at a yard sale and not realized the immense value of it. Viola had treasured it, kept it in pristine condition, and reread it a thousand times. And reading it with Ruby made the poems come to life in the best way possible.

When Vi's mother stopped visiting around the holidays, Walt and Ruby helped her to celebrate without her. When she stopped calling, Walt's words came through loud and clear. And when Viola stood at the precipice of adulthood, trying to navigate her most important relationships, she had darn near every page of *Leaves of Grass* memorized, with the only important memories of her mother being colored in dark blue disappointment.

Perhaps Viola even owed her romance career to Ruby for this. She valued the ability to write her own heroes, take charge of her own stories. If love was unreliable and pernicious in the real world, then she could right its wrongs on paper. She could expose romance for what it was. In being the best sister and the best kind of friend, Ruby had taught her that. Of course, her recent books had lost that romantic view of romance as she recycled old clichés and revisited tired tropes, but she still credited Ruby for her push into writing romance.

Wedding season and all its annoyances be damned, the least that Viola could do for Ruby was to be her Maid of Honor. She'd wear the dress, the heels, and a big, cheesy smile that never revealed to her sister's wedding guests that she didn't necessarily buy into the institution herself.

Ruby sighed, relieved and pleased. "Lovely. You can be my Maid of Honor, and I can be yours when we *finally* get you partnered up."

"Ugh, if you're going to try to set me up again, then I take back my acceptance." Viola turned on the hot shower and plopped down on the counter. "Jean-Luc is all the man I need; thank you very much."

"But you've got that big apartment and the fancy job and you're looking so beautiful lately. All you need now is—"

"Flattery will get you nowhere, *Mom*," Viola said. "You know how I feel about the lovey-dovey junk. Jean-Luc stays on the page where he belongs."

Her eyes fell on the blue toothbrush still stored by her bathroom sink. Matt had left it there when she broke up with him over a month ago. It wasn't her wanting him back, though, that had kept it sitting there for so long. It wasn't nostalgia, either, or a sense of wanton romance. It was her own lack of cleanliness and organization, plain and simple. Voila picked it up and tossed it in the small trashcan by the toilet.

She was happy for Ruby and Scott. She was happy for Hannah, her funny, independent best friend who had found an even greater joy in life after she met Aaron. But Viola didn't believe in love, not for herself anyway. She could write the best romances because she knew their cadences, their patterns. They were easy to predict and even easier to leave behind when she was done with them.

"Fine," Ruby finally conceded with a little laugh. "See you tonight?"

"You bet," Viola agreed.

Chapter 2

The Post Malone blasting through the chapel was definitely going to date this wedding.

Viola couldn't help but roll her eyes as its beat pounded through the little chapel. Still, she had to admit that the hip hop music seemed worth playing, since Hannah and Aaron were dancing their way through the practice ceremony, laughing and joking together in a world all their own. Viola herself even managed to muster a little side-step to the beat as Ruby egged her on from next to her in the long line of bridesmaids.

After the final vows were rehearsed and the group was released to the restaurant down the street for dinner, Hannah had found Viola. She hooked a skinny, freckled arm around her shoulders and grinned. "This is unreal," Hannah breathed, her thick Georgia accent magically dragging the last word out into three syllables. She looked starry-eyed and out of breath with excitement.

"You're telling me," agreed Viola. "I can still remember you planning your wedding to Jimmy Capriotti back when we were in elementary school. You're not old enough to be a real bride."

"Do you think Aaron would be offended if I called off the weddin' to hold out for Jimmy? That gapped-tooth smile still does things to me." Hannah grinned, joking.

It really did feel unreal to Viola. She'd known Hannah for as long as she'd known her own sister, Ruby, and it felt like her friend was the honorary third sister in their group. She'd been the next-door neighbor when Viola and her father had moved in with Andrea's family, and Viola could remember countless nights spent decoding flashlight Morse code through their windows or staying up late to camp out in one of their backyards.

In their youth, Hannah Anderson had been a wild child, her electric blossom of red hair and face full of freckles the perfect compliments to her upbeat and adventurous personality. As a grown woman, she still had the red hair and freckles, but she had been smoothed around the edges, molded into the kind of professional who wore her hair in a smart curled bob around her shoulders and bought expensive makeup to make the freckles appear more like a mature style detail. As a bride, Hannah looked even more like an adult, suddenly appearing to Viola as far older than herself, even though Hannah was actually a year younger.

Suddenly, Viola felt a punch to the gut; she had a renewed realization that Hannah's marriage meant that both girls were moving on from their carefree childhood days.

Viola liked Aaron. He was a good old Southern boy, about as good as any bride could ask for with his volunteering on the weekends and the rotating rounds of adopted dogs he fostered. Darn near a saint, albeit one with a penchant for dirty jokes. But giving her Hannah up to him felt like Viola was giving up some vital part of herself. Her friend's romance had given Hannah something new and special and wonderful—and had taken something away from Viola.

The girls walked in tandem to the restaurant, their arms still hooked around one another. Vi's fingers were quivering, a sure indicator that her stress level was rising. She hoped there would be booze served.

As soon as she had the thought, she winced. Viola might be a cynic, but she still felt bad that her first instinct was to drown out a night of her best friend's romance and sappy love stories with alcohol. She wanted to be fully present for every aspect of the wedding. She wanted to support Hannah and show her that she loved her. But still, she couldn't help but feel like a fish out of water. She belonged on the other side of this world, writing about it from a distance where she could safely dissect romance and passion and call it out for what it was nine times out of ten: frivolous distraction.

They entered the restaurant together, where the rest of the group was already waiting. Aaron, Hannah's tall, dark, and bearded betrothed, swooped in.

"So sorry to take you away from your first love, darlin'." His accent was as thick as Hannah's and even more dreamy. Aaron smiled and winked at Viola. "Duty calls. We start the toasts in a few minutes, and I need you back at our table."

Hannah slipped her hand into Viola's and squeezed before heading off with Aaron. "Ugh, it's just so hard to be the center of attention," she called, feigning dramatics. The other guests laughed, unable to resist Hannah's charm.

Viola sized up the rest of the room. Ruby and Scott were seated near the bride and groom's table. Her sister stood up, waving her over to join them.

Viola had just taken her first steps in their direction

when she felt a heavy hand on her shoulder. She turned to find her father with Wife Number Four standing before her.

"Sweet pea," he began. "Were you headed off to Roo's table? That's where we're seated, too."

"Yep. Great." Viola said through gritted teeth. Her sour mood deepened.

Wife Number Four was tall, curvy, and young. The most interesting thing about her were her long, thick eyelash extensions that fluttered too much when she talked. She was the perfect, superficial compliment to Viola's father, a real estate professional who had always cared more about the brand of his clothes and the gray in his beard than his own daughter. Viola had only met this wife once, at her father's quick wedding at the local courthouse.

Viola had wondered then if she had met the familiar-looking bride back in high school. She didn't dare ask her father for confirmation of step-mommy's age. There were some things she never wanted to know.

"Wasn't the venue just lovely?" Wifey asked, the eyelash extensions sent into a flurry once more. *Was her name Sabrina? Stephanie?* Viola struggled to remember. She also struggled to care. "I wish Dan and I had gotten married in a church. Maybe for our vow renewal." She giggled.

"I'll look forward to that invite," Viola said dryly. She started back toward Ruby's table, leading the trio.

Viola could already imagine how her sister would chastise her for her treatment of her father. Dan Reed might be a self-absorbed womanizer, but Ruby was quick to point out that he was the parent who hadn't given up his daughter. He had stuck by Viola's side, and maybe that was worth a little grace. Even if he hadn't parented particularly well.

"Viola! Dan! I'm so glad to see some familiar faces." Ruby smiled warmly, hugging Viola's father before turning to his new wife. "And you must be Sandra. I've heard so many good things about you."

"*I haven't*," Viola muttered under her breath to Scott, Ruby's fiancé. "They won't be together long enough for me to learn anything more than the name of her divorce attorney."

Scott stifled a laugh and elbowed Viola as a silent admonishment. He stuck out his hand for Sandra to shake. "Nice to meet you, Sandra. And always good to see you, Dan. We were so excited to hear about your marriage."

There was a sparkle in Scott's eye. Viola had gotten to know him well enough that she knew one of his cheesy jokes was coming.

"Hey, do you know why melons have weddings?" he asked, smile beaming. When the group didn't answer, instead casting knowing looks at each other, he shrugged and declared, "Because they *cantaloupe!*"

"Ha!" Dan barked and elbowed his new wife, who looked rather annoyed at the gesture. "Isn't he a hoot, darling?"

Viola couldn't help it: she felt a twinge of affection toward her father. Four wives and bills for six different divorce attorneys hadn't dampened his goofy sense of humor. Maybe Ruby had a point; Viola should soften up a bit and give him a chance. God knew she could use a little humor in her life these days.

Scott was still laughing to himself as the group started off to their seats. Ruby swatted at him as if the line should have annoyed her, but Viola could see the irresistible smile already overtaking her lips. Ruby loved Scott's dad jokes and boisterous nature. They were the perfect complement to her introversion, her preciousness, her sometimes too-serious demeanor. Scott really brought out the best in Ruby.

Watching them together sometimes gave Viola that little spark inside her chest that made her want to sit down with her laptop and get to writing. Their relationship seemed so real, so attainable. She wanted so badly to capture it on paper. Ruby and Scott's relationship almost made her believe in the reality of an easy love.

Almost.

Scott pulled out a chair for his fiancée and then stepped forward to pull out a chair for Sandra as well. "After you, m'lady," he cracked with a smile.

Viola was baffled by how Ruby and Scott could maintain such a good relationship with her father and this wife-of-the-week. Dan had been married to Andrea for a grand total of four years before bailing for his pretty young secretary, and yet Ruby persisted as the kind of ex-stepdaughter who still wrote him Father's Day cards and called to wish him a happy birthday. It was likely more respect and care than Viola herself gave to him.

"Well, shall we?" Viola gestured to her father to sit down next to her. She was eager to get dinner going and start drinking the rest of the night away.

The rest of them took their seats. Ruby leaned in towards Viola, putting a hand on her knee. "We got them a spa gift card," she said, looking worried. "Do you think that's enough?"

"I think Hannah will love it," Viola smiled, taking her sister's hand to squeeze it. "And it's about a million times more thoughtful than the rice cooker I opted for."

Scott leaned in to join them with a wicked grin. "Vi, if you plan on getting us a rice cooker for our wedding, then you're getting uninvited. I'll be accepting lingerie or nothing."

Ruby threw back her head and laughed, clutching Viola's knee.

Her sister looked so happy these days. She had met Scott at a corporate event, and he'd charmed her with tales of his bass fishing on Lake Lanier gone bad. They'd been inseparable ever since. Bought the small house with the cherry blossom tree out front and the porch swing out back—the rest was history.

Viola felt the pang again as she thought of her precious Ruby leaving her the way Hannah was. For the life of her, she couldn't understand how these girls weren't terrified of the futures they were forging. Weren't they aware of the divorce rate? The Ashley Madison accounts? Or—worst of all—the passion dying out? Viola had written about all of it enough times to feel like she'd lived out several lifetimes' worth of her own marriages. Sure, her stories had happy endings, but she was too smart to believe them. She scooted closer to her sister, putting an arm around her shoulders and holding her tight as the toasts began. Her fingers were still quivering, and she sent out a silent prayer that they would stop as they found Ruby's skin. She didn't want that kind of future for her precious Ruby, but there was nothing for her to do.

Aaron was standing up at the couple's table, one hand lovingly placed on Hannah's shoulder as he raised his glass. "Thanks for comin', everyone," he called out.

His grin was big and toothy; he looked downright giddy. Despite Aaron's carefully combed hair and impeccable tuxedo that he wore now, Viola's mind instantly flashed back to when she met him during college. He'd worn the same big grin when he picked Hannah up from the girls' apartment for their first date, and he'd worn it all week after Hannah had let him kiss her for the first time behind the science building.

"The rehearsal dinner is officially behind us, which means this wedding is half over and you can all stop spending ridiculous amounts of money on us soon."

The guests all laughed. Hannah made a big waving motion to the crowd, as though it were necessary to assure them that he was kidding. Viola caught her friend's eye and sent a clandestine wink her way, knowing full well that her best friend relished in the opportunity to have the full, grand Southern wedding experience... ridiculous amounts of monetary gifts definitely included.

Aaron let his hand slip down onto the bare spot on Hannah's back, where her silky pink dress had slipped down off of her shoulders. His fingertips lingered there, rubbing the skin with the barest, most delicate touch. "To my future bride," he said simply, throwing back his drink to finish the toast.

"To your future bride," Viola echoed with the group. She took a deep sip of the wine, already finishing off her glass. She could feel Ruby's eyes on her as she raised a hand to flag down a waiter for a refill.

Aaron picked Viola out in the crowd, waving her up to join him. "Vi, you're up!"

Viola stood up, feeling a little unsteady on her feet as she took in the dozens of faces that were watching her. She picked her way over to the bride and groom's table, silently cursing Ruby for talking her into wearing heels. She took the mic from Aaron and cleared her throat.

"Hey, everyone." Feedback screeched out loud and whiny. Viola winced, pulling the mic back for a moment. She steeled herself once more and brought it back to her face. "Hey. I'm Viola. Vi. Sometimes Vee. I don't know why I said that; nobody ever calls me that…"

A ripple of laughter went through the crowd as Viola cleared her throat, trying to regain her composure. She realized then that her hands were sweating. The mic was slipping around in her fingers. She tightened up her grip and reached into her pocket to pull out her planned speech.

The words staring back at her didn't feel right. They were canned, an empty reflection on all the lovey-dovey couples that Viola wrote about in her books. Suddenly they didn't seem worthy of her sweet best friend and the genuine, adoring way that Aaron was looking at Hannah right now. She couldn't use this; she needed to nail down what their relationship was really all about. Viola pocketed the paper and looked up into the waiting faces. Her heartbeat quickened as she realized that ditching her planned toast meant that she'd be on her own.

Hannah was staring at her, her face expectant. She smiled encouragingly and gestured subtly to Viola: *Move on.*

"Um, when Hannah told me that she was getting married, I told her that she was nuts." Viola stumbled over the words. "I mean, we all know the statistics. Like, forty percent of marriages end in divorce, with each marriage after having an even stronger likelihood of ending badly. It's like, does true love even exist? Does the risk involved even make it worth having?"

She paused, realizing that not only was she rambling, but now the crowd was starting to get a bit uncomfortable. Hannah was pulling back the high collar of her dress, airing out what was surely a hot neck. Viola straightened up, remembering the purpose of a rehearsal dinner toast.

"But then I look at Hannah and Aaron, and the risk doesn't really feel that big anymore. Their love story isn't all starry nights and candlelit dinners or all that other stuff you see in the movies. It's more real. It's Aaron hand-making Hannah chicken and dumplings when she had the flu last winter. It's Hannah taking the time to teach Aaron how to properly take care of a Christmas tree after he nearly burnt down our college apartment that one time."

"Keep insultin' me and I won't be invitin' you to my second wedding either, Vi," Aaron joked. The crowd laughed again.

Viola smiled, feeling the tension that she'd experienced as she started her toast beginning to melt away. There was truth in what she was saying. Maybe Aaron and Hannah had a real chance together. If anyone deserved a good love story, it was them.

"These two people love each other, and they're about to make the leap and commit their lives to one another," Viola commended. "I think it's brave. I think it's admirable. And maybe I'm even a little jealous that Hannah will get to eat that homemade chicken and dumplings for the rest of her life. To Aaron and Hannah: may their marriage be long and prosperous."

"To Aaron and Hannah!" The crowd repeated happily before knocking back their drinks. Aaron stood up.

"Now before we get into the rest of the toasts, let's get that Post Malone pumping again," Aaron announced. "This is a party!"

Viola smiled and cheered along with everyone else. The toast hadn't gone too badly. If she could handle this, maybe she could handle the onslaught of upcoming weddings this year. She only had a finite number of eligible sorority sisters, right? Wedding season would have to end, eventually. And in the meantime, maybe she could even find a few things to enjoy about the festivities.

Chapter 3

The reception hall was packed to capacity. Viola had helped Aaron and Hannah to set up the venue the night before. She'd been throwing back the rehearsal dinner wine pretty heavily, though, and hadn't realized at the time just how claustrophobic the mountains of greenery and the low-strung fairy lights would make her feel. The crowd seemed to be pulsing around her, and she felt like she was drowning in the middle of a vast ocean of writhing bodies. Viola stayed close to the wall as she shuffled in, hoping that she would blend in with the lavender and navy décor.

She recognized faces from her alma mater in passing. Old hallmates were there with husbands and even the occasional child. Aaron's fraternity brothers were impossible to miss congregated by the open bar. They were the other half of all those Facebook engagements she'd been seeing: the deer-huntin', beer-drinkin' Southern boys that were obligated to marry all of those sorority sisters and supply them with 2.5 picture-perfect children.

Hannah just *had* to go all starry-eyed over one of the most popular guys at college; he must have invited half the school. Viola would have preferred to be at a smaller venue. Let's be real, she admitted to herself: she would prefer to be at home, drinking wine alone with Duncan. Once more, she checked the little card she'd been issued with her table number. Sixteen.

Hannah must have apologized for the inconvenience right up until the minute she had walked down the aisle. The makeup artist had made no small display of showing how annoying it was to try to cover thousands of freckles with concealer as Hannah kept turning to tell Viola that the singles' table was Aaron's idea, definitely not hers. Her thick mane of kinky red curls kept obscuring her eyelids, sending the makeup artist into a near conniption fit.

But, trying her best to be the dutiful Maid of Honor and feeling keenly aware of Ruby as another bridesmaid watching for signs that her sister wouldn't ruin her own wedding, Viola sucked it up, took the table card, and committed herself to an evening of misery in socializing. How many singles could Aaron and Hannah know, anyway?

"You lost?"

Viola turned at the feeling of a hand on her elbow, near-instantly irritated. A stranger stood before her, wearing a funny little half-smile.

She knew this type of guy well. His kind was at every wedding, using the same pickup lines and preying on the same lonely singles. Viola wondered how many women he would have had to approach and strike out with before lowering himself to approaching the disheveled girl who was dressed in heavily wrinkled silk and clearly drinking straight whiskey.

Still, she had to admit that he took the role and ran with it. He was suave and confident; she could tell that straight away. With a thick, curling mop of dark hair, a strong, broad nose, and ears that jutted out just a bit too far, she would have thought him average in passing. But he was clearly one who put in a little effort. He wore a slick, tailored black suit, complete with perfectly placed bow tie. The smell of his cologne, nutty and spiced, was subtle but distinct. She even noticed tiny cufflinks, shaped like miniature tigers. She would guess that his pickup lines probably had a little more success than those of the average wedding charmer.

Viola resented the blush that crept up on her cheeks. *You caught me off guard, buddy.* She thought. *Don't think this routine works on me.* She withdrew her arm and brandished her card.

"Table sixteen?" she asked.

He produced his own card and smiled again. "Looks like we're table buddies." *Hooray.* He extended a hand to lead her to their spot. "I'm Brooks Hardison. The groom and I were frat brothers."

"Viola Reed," she said, curt. "Maid of Honor."

"I remember," Brooks said. "I noticed you during the service. I thought that bridesmaids weren't allowed to look better than the bride."

"Oh, come on." Viola laughed despite herself. They had found their table, and she pulled out a chair next to two singles whose flushed cheeks and goo-goo eyes indicated zero interest in their new table companions. Vi sat down and propped her elbows up on the table as she cocked an eyebrow at him. "Does that line really work for you?"

Brooks looked taken aback. "I'm serious!" He sat down beside her, reaching a hand out to gently brush off a stray cat hair from her shoulder. "That dress is really something. You have that... that..."

"Je ne sais quoi?" she supplied, her brow pinched in skepticism. "That thing that gives you the butterflies? That indescribable quality that makes you believe in rainbows and unicorns?"

Brooks folded his arms and leaned back, sizing her up. "Go on; don't let me stop you."

Viola smiled, starting to feel more than a little cocky. "You just touched my shoulder, right? Physical touch is a great way to build a connection. It tricks the brain into thinking there's a natural intimacy between two people. You've got the right suit, too, with all the little details. So clearly you came prepared. And you didn't sign up for a plus-one, or you wouldn't be camped out at the singles' table like me. It's obvious: you're trolling for a hook-up."

He laughed and leaned forward to take a swig of his drink. "You've done this before."

"I'm a romance novelist." she shrugged, smiling. "Writer by day, killer of joy by night."

Brooks put his hands up as though he'd been caught. "Alright, you got me. But can you blame me? Weddings are perfect for finding a pretty face or two. And between all the fraternity brothers I had back in college, I've been starting to attend a *lot* of weddings lately."

"Ugh," Viola could relate. "Haven't any of them heard of elopement?"

"I think that Southern mamas consider that to be a dirty word," Brooks grinned. "I keep getting enticed to come to these things with the promise that some perfect, single girl named Emily is going to show up and sweep me off my feet. I'm starting to think that my friends all got together and made her up to trick me. Have you seen any Emilys?"

They were interrupted by the squealing feedback of a microphone. They turned to see Hannah's father taking the stage, waving for the band to quiet down.

"Thank you for coming everyone!" The guests whooped

and hollered, raising their drinks in excitement. "If everyone could gather by the buffet, the happy couple is going to cut their cake."

Viola and Brooks got up from their chairs, making their way through the pulsing crowd to watch the event. Brooks leaned in toward her, and she got another hit of his heady cologne. She shimmied away, trying to put a little distance between them.

"Okay, it's my turn to show off," he whispered to her. "You might be able to predict romance, but I can predict the weddings."

Viola found a spot behind Aaron's nieces and nephews, who clamored over each other to get a good view of the cake. Brooks settled in next to her, clearly committed to his routine. She sighed.

Following a change in the music, Hannah and Aaron emerged through the throng, smiling and waving. Viola thought her friend looked like a dream. With her titian hair pulled into a sophisticated knot and her green eyes shining in contrast to the creamy ruffles of her white sleeves and collar, she looked positively angelic, and the glow of her happy smile at her new spouse made her look all the more radiant. Viola was surprised at the small pang she felt in her chest as she watched her best friend pick up the silver cake cutting knife.

"Okay," Brooks started, grounding her back in reality. "Vanilla cake is milquetoast, but it's perfect for the bride trying to please everyone. Chocolate is a step in a fancier direction, but I happen to know that Aaron can't stand the stuff. Fruity or exotic flavors are for the adventurous or the outright kooky. And red velvet is reserved for themed weddings, Christmas or a macabre Halloween. I'd bet we've got a vanilla on our hands."

"You're on," Viola said, grudgingly accepting the challenge. "You clearly don't know much about Hannah. She ate live crickets on her Study Abroad. There's nothing vanilla about her."

The pair paused as Aaron took Hannah's arms, guiding her to cut into the flowery desert. Viola watched with bated breath as her giggling friend picked up a piece before smashing it into her husband's face. White cake flew everywhere. Viola winced, defeated.

"I'm basically a psychic." Brooks was grinning.

"Come on, like 50% of wedding cakes must be vanilla." She chided, a hand on her hip. "You got lucky."

He put his hands in the air, the picture of innocence. "All I do is observe and report. I saw the themed cocktails back at the bar and knew this was going to be a Basic Bitch wedding."

"Ouch, definitely going to have to report that back to Hannah."

Brooks shrugged, slipping his hands in his pockets. "Come on. 'Bloody Marry Me?' 'Old Fashioned Love Story?' 'Mint-To-Be Julep?' Embarrassing."

"Alright; it's pretty awful." Viola agreed, chuckling.

"Father-daughter dance is up next, right?" Brooks was eyeballing the band stand.

Hannah's father had returned to the stage once more, his announcement perfectly timed with Brooks' assumption. "Okay, I'm listening," Viola said.

"Safe bets for a father-daughter dance are usually 'I Loved Her First,' 'Butterfly Kisses,' or 'Your Song.' But I think your girl Hannah's dad looks pretty spry so I'm putting my money on 'Jump On It.' Brace for cheesy choreography."

A slow song queued up as Hannah met her father on the dance floor. He took her in his arms and pulled her close.

"Someone is getting a little too big for his britches," Viola laughed, elbowing Brooks. "You're lucky we didn't put money down—"

The song shifted. The iconic beat of The Sugarhill Gang's drums cut through the room as the guests went wild. Viola's mouth dropped despite herself; how could he have known? Through the crowd, Hannah's eyes found Viola's, and she tossed her the bouquet before hiking up her skirt and joining her father in a goofy routine.

"I might need to hire you to come write for me," Viola said to Brooks, impressed. "You're good at this."

She couldn't help it; her interest was fully piqued. Viola rarely found herself surprised by anyone, but especially not by the kind of young men who wore fancy suits and used more hair product than she did. Brooks Hardison was supposed to be the kind of character who was simply sleazy and aggressive, or at least flat, empty-headed, and an irritating conversationalist. She certainly didn't expect to find him so funny.

The pair headed back to their table, narrowly avoiding drunken dancing couples. Viola found her seat, where an entrée had been left in her absence by the waiting staff. Her stomach rumbled. She stashed the bouquet at the center of the table and sat down.

"I'm ravenous," she said, picking up her fork to dig into her meal.

Brooks sat down next to her and loosened his tie before picking up his drink to take a swallow. "So how good is the romance book business exactly?" He asked her, looking interested. "Should I quit my day job in finance and come work for you?"

"It's not too shabby," she said. "Difficult initially, but if you put in the work to earn the trust of some real fans, then you're pretty much set. Besides, everyone wants escapism when they read. It's why the non-fiction section of Barnes and Noble looks dusty while sci-fi and fantasy books are dog-eared."

"Hold up; I read non-fiction."

She snorted. "Not with a suit like that you don't. *Maybe* a sports biography or coffee table book, but nothing more serious than Dave Ramsey's titles. Or wait—" she laughed out loud, delighted by her own brilliance, "—maybe you just subscribe to *Mad Magazine* or *Playboy.*"

"Jokes on you." Looking mock offended, Brooks reached into his deep pockets, producing a small, weathered copy of Stephen Hawking's *A Brief History of Time.*

Viola was floored. It wasn't often someone defied her expectations to this extent. Usually, they might do something out of character once or twice, but never this much. "Well, dang, Hardison, you keep the surprises coming."

"... And I might also have a subscription to *Mad Magazine* that comes to my apartment."

Viola laughed so hard that her drink shot out of her nose. She winced, her nostrils burning, as Brooks offered her a handkerchief from his jacket.

"Are you for real?" She asked, brandishing the cloth square. "I honestly thought they stopped making these at the turn of the century."

Brooks shrugged and smiled. "Alright, Viola Reed. You've successfully convinced me that you're not wedding bait. Are there any other single guests you'd recommend for me? I've been to enough weddings to know that I prefer not to leave them alone."

She glanced around at the rest of their lonely singles' table. Outside of the two lovebirds next to Viola's seat, it seemed that Brooks' only other options there were a woman at least twice his age or a young man wearing a *Futurama* tie. She shrugged and speared a bite of food.

"I generally prefer cats to people," she said through a mouthful of chicken and broccoli. "Consequently, I have no good recommendations for you."

"It is a wonder you're here alone," Brooks pronounced with a laugh. "Well, at least tell me which of your friends is a good dancer. I need to hit the dance floor soon or I'll lose my mind."

"Sorry," Viola shrugged and took another bite. "If I found your Zack Morris routine more enticing, maybe I'd come dance with you. I'm the best one here. I have a weird passion for swing dancing; it fits in great with my single-cat-lady-hermit persona."

"You're really breaking my heart here." Brooks put a hand to his chest. "Not to worry, I think I just found my own partner, anyway."

He stood up as a tall, twiggy blonde in a short gold dress walked by, her eyes searching over the crowd.

"You lost?" Brooks asked as he approached her. Their voices faded away as Viola watched him put a hand on the small of her back and guide her off to the dance floor. The blonde threw her head back in laughter, her big, round baby blue eyes shimmering as she complimented some joke Brooks had made.

The music shifted from "Jump On It." The wedding band had returned to the stage, taking up their instruments to play a bold, brassy number. Well, fancy that. It was a swing dance.

Viola watched as Brooks led the blonde in the dance. She looked markedly less graceful as her feet fumbled over his and her back stayed stiff and straight. She was still laughing, but her smile looked pained as she tried to keep up.

Brooks, on the other hand, was still all suave and control. He guided the girl with expert precision, helping her to each step and catching her when she started to fall. He had definitely done this before.

Viola couldn't help it—her foot started tapping under the table. She had successfully spent every wedding thus far peacefully and individually raiding the buffet table for thousand calorie snacks and abusing the open bar policy. This wedding just had to play some swing music the one time another sad sack single was around to badger her.

"Ugh," Viola murmured out loud, chewing down one last bite of her delicious chicken. She couldn't take it anymore: she resigned herself to looking like every other desperate wedding single out there. She got up from the table and headed out to the dance floor.

She tapped on the blonde's shoulder. "Can I cut in?"

The girl looked grateful as she stepped aside. Viola took Brooks' hand and stepped close. His eyebrows were raised in surprise.

"Don't think your little scheme worked on me," she said as she started to kick and jump to the rhythm. "I just can't resist a good swing dance."

"I'm not going to get to find a girl to go home with tonight, am I?" Brooks laughed.

Chapter 4

"So, let me get this straight: you're happy for Aaron and Hannah, you support their marriage, but somehow you still don't believe that love exists?"

Brooks and Viola had left the reception at midnight, wandering the streets of the city in search of late-night grub. She hated to admit it, but he had grown on her. They had danced for a long time, and Viola had been grateful for the excuse to turn down the many eager suitors that her sister had been sneakily sending her way all night. Brooks was a funny and nice guy, and he hadn't asked for her to pay a court debt for him, pretend to be his wife to impress his family, or murder a homeless person with him. Yet. All big pluses for male companionship.

Ever the smooth operator, he had even lent Viola his suit coat, which she pressed tight around her shoulders to keep out the evening chill. When she stumbled in her towering heels over the uneven brick of the downtown streets, he caught her by the elbow.

If she was really being honest, she might admit that she outright enjoyed Brooks' company. He was funny and insightful and made for a great dance partner. Viola knew, however, the conversations with Hannah and Ruby that were sure to follow any adventure out with a new man, and she had wanted to make sure he knew where she stood. So she'd laid out her life philosophy for him on the search to find a midnight snack, explaining just how it was that she could write about romance but not buy into it.

She shrugged, brushing herself off. "I believe that people *think* they're in love. And maybe they really are. They do all sorts of crazy things for it, like starting wars or cutting off family members. But it's not like in the movies. And I don't think it's lasting. I think it's kind of foolish to pursue it so hard."

Viola was well aware of how jaded she sounded. But as she said the words aloud, she still couldn't help but picture the father with commitment problems and the mother who would rather trade up for a new family than love the one she had. Come on, even Ruby's picture-perfect mother Andrea had gone through a divorce. It was hard for Vi to have any life philosophy that didn't echo her lonely upbringing. All good things had an expiration date, at least she was realistic about it.

"So, what?" Brooks asked. He pointed at a Chinese restaurant down the street and led her forward. "You just don't date people?"

"Even the best of us need company that isn't feline or Netflix," she laughed. "I do date people. I had a boyfriend off and on last year."

"What happened?" he asked.

She ran a hand through her hair, thinking. "He wanted to get serious, and I just wanted a good friend. We had different relationship goals. One of us would have been miserable in the end, so I cut it off when I could."

Brooks opened the door to the restaurant and gestured for Viola to head inside. The warmth of the dining room blasted out at her and she gratefully shimmied off his suit coat. They found a table at the back, making themselves at home with the menus as they waited on a lone, exhausted waitress to come over and take their orders.

"That was an incredibly depressing relationship story," he declared. "With that attitude, you're practically begging the universe to send you someone to come sweep you off your feet and break your heart."

"So you believe in true love yourself then?" she asked him, one eyebrow raised as she thumbed through the menu. "Mr. 'Different Bridesmaid at Every Wedding?'"

Brooks grinned unashamedly and put a hand on his heart. "I've been in love a thousand times!" he jested. "It's just that none of them have turned out to be my Cinderella yet. But that could all change if you came back with me to my apartment after we eat here..." He waggled his eyebrows in a comic invitation.

Viola tossed her menu at him, smiling as it smacked him in the chest. "Dream on." She crossed her arms and sat back in her chair, sizing him up. "Unfortunately for you, my history as a romance novelist has informed me that the likelihood of you ever finding Cinderella is zero to none."

"Oh, is this your superpower again? Pray tell me why I don't deserve happiness."

The waitress had finally made it over to their table. With her hair in a messy bun at the top of her head, her apron stained with unidentifiable greases, and her uniform reeking of cigarette smoke, it seemed apparent that she would rather be anywhere else. Unsmiling and grim, she pulled out a tiny wrinkled pad, jotted down their orders without any questions, and trotted off to the kitchen, leaving them alone once more.

Viola put up her hands, squinting and framing Brooks as though he were a picture. "You're the classic playboy trope," she started. "You're not devastatingly handsome enough to be the leading man."

"Wow, hurtful. But go on."

Viola laughed and continued. "You're clearly not a villain, because the girls you take home from weddings don't seem to be in committed relationships and, while your humor is biting, I doubt you've pissed off anyone too much in your past. You're too suave and charming to be the best friend type. And, as far as I can tell, you're no one significant's father or brother."

"*That we know of*," Brooks joked. "I'm still worried that Ancestry.com will come back to bite me with some illegitimate children one day."

Viola smiled, shaking her head. "If I had to guess, I'd say that in a romance novel, you'd be the guy who flirts with all the women. A plot device used to make the leading man jealous or perhaps to distract the leading lady from her ultimate love. You'll date a bunch of women, but never get close enough to any of them for true love. You'll have some fun while you're young and still good-looking, but ultimately you won't win the big prize. No Cinderella for you." Viola shrugged indifferently as she settled back in her seat, waiting for his reaction to her prediction.

The waitress returned with two sweating glasses of water. Brooks took his and gulped down a massive swig, clearly needing it. He sat back in his chair, running a hand through his unruly dark curls. He shook his head at Viola.

"Wow, you cut me to my core." He took another drink and then set down the glass, closing his eyes and pinching the bridge of his nose while he thought. "I hate to admit how much of that sounds accurate. So, I'm the playboy. But you're leading lady material, I assume?"

"Hardly," Viola snorted and took a sip of her own water. "Quirky side friend, at *best*."

"How do you figure?"

"Brooks, you're talking to a woman who is in her late twenties, lives alone, and proudly claims a cat as her closest companion. And if that wasn't enough, I'm a quarter Native. Minorities don't get leading lady status, thank you racist America. *Maybe* if I was Black or Latina, but—"

Brooks shook his head, that funny little half smile returning to his face. "Reed, I think you might be the worst cynic I've ever met."

"I am what I am," she smiled and raised her glass in a mocking salute.

"Honestly, I kind of wish I shared your perspective." He admitted, swirling his cup around, making the ice cubes rattle against the plastic. "I fall hard, and I fall fast. Meaning my mother gets the son who dates all of her friend's daughters but marries absolutely none of them. It must be relaxing not to constantly pursue a relationship."

"Or you could just try monogamy." Viola teased with a smile.

The waitress returned once more, various egg rolls and noodles piled high on dubiously clean plates. They took the dishes from her and divvied out the goods to share between them.

Viola took her first bite of noodles and veggies. She moaned with ecstasy. "You've got to try this."

"Jeez, Reed, you're kind of making me want to hook up with the lo mein next." Brooks laughed, spearing his own portion to take a bite.

"So, tell me," Viola started, her mouth still half-full of noodles. "How do you pick your prey?"

"Not prey," he corrected her. "I'm a romantic, not an animal. I just try a little bit of everything. The preppy girls, the wild ones, even the losers."

He winked at her, and she flicked some lo mein in his direction. "But really," Brooks went on, his voice getting softer, more serious. Something dark flashed across his face. "I've learned that people can surprise you. For the good and the bad. If I'm going to commit to someone, I want to be sure of who they are. So in the meantime, I'm giving everyone a chance. All chicks created equal."

"You're a pig," Viola chastised, rolling her eyes.

"And you're growing to like it." He grinned rakishly.

Viola felt a buzz in her pocket. She pulled her phone from her pocket. *RUBY*. She groaned, realizing immediately what she had forgotten.

"I'm sorry; I better wrap this meal up kind of fast," she explained to Brooks. He looked up at her with his own mouthful of lo mein, brow furrowed. "My sister is calling to make sure I got in for the night. She's probably worried that I've forgotten about the post-wedding brunch with Aaron and Hannah tomorrow morning ... which I did."

She glanced at the time and winced. *One a.m.* Her gut was going to pay for these noodles in the morning. She was too old to be acting like she was 21 again. Still, she couldn't help but feel grateful for the promise of a little brunch champagne to nurse the headache she would inevitably have in the morning.

Brooks waved at the waitress, motioning for a box for their food. "This was fun," he said. "After a wedding, I usually prefer picking up exotic women over exotic food, but I'll admit that this wasn't so bad. Maybe I'll catch you at another wedding sometime."

"'Tis the season," Viola said, offering her hand for him to shake as she stood up from the table.

"Tell Aaron hello for me," he said. "I never got to check in with him at the reception. And try not to talk too much about how all relationships are doomed from the get-go, okay? Kinda puts a damper on pancakes and eggs."

"I make no promises." She smiled at him and pushed in her chair.

Viola made her way through the maze of chairs and tables to the exit, where a gaggle of drunken college girls were coming inside. "Is this Chinese food or whaaat?" One of the girls slurred, holding out the last word a bit too long. Her friends collapsed into giggles.

Viola pushed past them to go through the door. "You lost?" She mouthed with a smile as she heard Brooks standing up to greet them.

Had she just accidentally made a new friend that wasn't her sister, her longtime best friend, or—gasp—an animal? Viola found that she was happy for herself tonight, too. The wedding hadn't been as bad as she'd thought.

Chapter 5

Hannah was choking on her eggs benedict.

The post-wedding brunch had started normally enough, with all the awkward pleasantries that were to be expected after the first night a happy couple spent together as official husband and wife. Viola had found a seat at the long table beside Ruby and Scott and hidden herself as a recluse as Hannah's parents chatted up the fraternity boys and sorority sisters who sat at the other end of seats.

Over sparkling champagne, they'd talked about the success of the reception, the first round of gifts the pair had opened in the morning, and the plans for the rest of the weekend. Just after the food had arrived, Hannah had asked Viola where she'd gone after the dancing. She'd taken a big bite of her eggs benedict as Vi explained that she'd headed out to find food with Brooks Hardison.

Aaron had guffawed as he smacked his new wife on the back, his mouth split into a ridiculous grin. Hannah's face had turned as red as her hair, her freckles jumping out in angry spots on her cheeks. She wiped her mouth with her napkin and turned back to Viola.

"You did not," she pronounced.

"Cat Lady Viola hooked up with Hardly Committed Hardison," Aaron laughed again. He raised a hand. "Gimme five, darlin'."

Hannah smacked her groom's hand away, annoyed. She put two fingers to her temples, rubbing. She looked remarkably like her own deeply Southern mama. With those two fingers working in a frenzy to rub away her stress, Vi could almost picture Hannah fretting over a torn pageant gown or worrying about the state of her magnolia tree compared to a neighbor's. "Tell me y'all didn't."

"Definitely not," Viola snorted. She took a bite of her own breakfast. The shredded potatoes were salty and delicious, just what she needed after a hangover and a late night. "We got Chinese food. That's it."

"That is never 'it' with Brooks Hardison," Hannah said. "I specifically had Aaron put him at the singles' table so that he would be isolated and away from all eligible guests. It was supposed to be Siberia over there."

"Hey, *I* was put at the singles' table." Viola raised an eyebrow at her friend and smirked.

"Hannah isn't exaggerating," Ruby commented, casually reaching for her water to take a sip. She tucked a loose blond curl behind her ear as she fixated her gaze on the cold glass. "I may have met him at a wedding once ... or twice."

Scott joined Aaron in laughter. "What can I say, it was before she met this king of romance over here. When we met, all I had to say was 'Well, here I am. Now what are your other two wishes?'" The boys highfived. Ruby rolled her eyes at another one of her fiancé's goofy dad jokes, but Viola could see her smiling in spite of her best efforts.

"But really, I knew Hardison in college, too," Scott continued. "Definitely a real playboy."

"Am I the only one who didn't meet this guy back at school?" Viola asked, taking another bite.

"Consider yourself spared," Hannah explained. "The man is like a tornado. He comes onto every girl he sees."

"Someone's bitter 'cause she never got a call back after *she* went out with him," Aaron explained, elbowing his new bride. "Hardison was a god in our fraternity. Dudes love him. *I* love him. But the ladies ... the ladies *hate* him." He laughed again.

"Completely undatable," Hannah agreed.

"Well, I didn't find him so objectionable." Viola shrugged.

Hannah waved her off. She reached over, picking up Vi's small plate bearing a freshly baked cinnamon roll. She forked off a large bite, dangling it in front of her friend's face. "Brooks is like this sugary treat," she explained. "Delicious—"

"Hey!" Aaron feigned offense, raising his hands.

"Definitely delicious," she affirmed, continuing. "He's sweet at first. Appealin'. You totally want to take a bite." Hannah popped the fork into her mouth, swallowing the cinnamon roll morsel. "But he'll rot your teeth."

"I did order that for myself, you know." Viola said, laughing.

"Get over it; I'm the one payin' for the brunch." Hannah smiled at her.

The group laughed as Viola stole her plate back, taking a bite of cinnamon roll herself. She moaned and slouched down in her seat as the sweet cream cheese frosting hit her tongue.

"This tastes amazing," she moaned. She paused her chewing, fork in hand. "Don't worry about me. There is more of a chance that I'll date this cinnamon roll than date

Brooks Hardison. He's just a friend." She picked up her fork and shoveled down another massive bite.

"Vi?"

It was Viola's turn to choke on her breakfast. She turned quickly in her chair, wishing to God that she would stop following the impulse to scarf down every fatty food she saw.

Matt stood before her, a hand on her chair. Her stomach dropped.

He looked the same as he had when Viola saw him last. His cool blue eyes were taking her in from under thick, dense dark eyebrows. He must have stopped shaving regularly, she thought; his swarthy stubble ran thick along his chiseled jaw line.

"Hey, Matt," Ruby waved.

"How are you?" Aaron asked from across the table.

A young woman, tall and reedy, approached him from behind, putting a hand to his shoulder. "We're at the table near the back," she told him with a smile. The girl took in the sight of the group and waved. She looked at Matt, expectant.

He shook his head as though to clear it. "I'm sorry," he started. "This is Rebecca. We work together."

The girl's smile faltered at the late introduction, but she recovered quickly. She waved at the group again, slipping away to greet her friends at a table nearby. "I'll order you some water," she called to him.

Matt made no move to leave, instead putting his hands in his pockets and shuffling his feet. It was an odd look for someone usually so confident and sure, Viola thought. She had only seen him this way once before.

Her fingers were already shaking again, and she felt a pang in her chest as she thought of Matt one month ago, sitting on the edge of her bed as she told him she didn't think it would work out between the two of them. He hadn't known what to say then either. He'd had the same look in his eyes, the same sad crease between his brows. He hadn't deserved to feel that way.

"Hey," she started, her voice hesitant and quiet. "We're just here for Hannah's brunch. Remember?"

"Course." Matt shook his head distractedly. He nodded at the couple. "Congratulations. I should really send you guys something."

"It's nothin', man." Aaron waved him off.

"Did you hear that Ruby's next?" Viola offered, gesturing to her sister.

Ruby smiled and waved at Matt, showing off the tiny sparkling diamond on her left ring finger. He smiled back and clapped Scott on the shoulder.

"Way to go," he said. "It's about time you make an honest woman out of this one."

His eyes darted back at Viola then. She felt that stab in her heart once more. She knew then that she had said the wrong thing, brought up the wrong subject.

"Hey, do you think I could have a sec, VI?" He asked, looking nervous.

"Of course," she stammered, awkwardly getting up from her chair to follow him across the dining room.

Matt stopped in a corner near the bathrooms, hands in his pockets and brow still furrowed. "Are you doing okay? Really?"

"Matt." Viola reached out and touched his arm. She pulled back just as quickly. Old habits. "It's me who should be checking in on you."

"You look tired. I really hope you're getting enough sleep. Wedding activities keeping you up?"

"My sequel, actually." As soon as she said the words, she regretted them. She could feel herself falling back into a familiar dance with Matt, into a conversation they'd had a million times before.

"You've got to cut yourself some slack," Matt said, reaching for her hand. She drew away, and he looked further pained.

"It's not a burden," she tried to explain. "I like the work."

"Writing isn't everything. Maybe I could call your agent for you. Or my sister is looking for a new English teacher at her charter school for next semester? Maybe you could—"

"Matt, I'm good." Viola affirmed. "Really."

He swallowed and shook his head. His eyes trained down on the floor. "Course." The silence hung heavy between them. "Well, I guess I ought to be getting back," Matt said finally. He nodded at her, his hands returning to his pockets. "It was great seeing you, Vi. I hope you stay well."

"You, too." She sent him a small smile as he turned and walked back to Rebecca and their group.

She hated that their interaction had been reduced down to the same conversation they'd been having their entire relationship. There were a million other things she would rather be talking to him about. What had he been doing over the past month? Had he moved back in with his roommates? With this new Rebecca, maybe? Had he started dating again? There were so many apps for that now. Matt would look great as a thumbnail.

Had he returned the ring? Viola felt sick to her stomach. In her mind's eye, she could still see it sparkling and shimmering in the little black box he had picked up off the counter on his way out her door. She wished so badly that he had never bought something like that. It was too late, though, and now she also wished that she could dispose of the memory with the same abandon as she had thrown out his toothbrush.

When Viola walked back to her own table, Hannah had crossed her arms, her eyebrows raised. "Okay, so if Brooks is Hardly Committed Hardison, then that one right there is definitely Born to Be Husband-Material Matt. Remind me why you're not the one getting hitched next?"

Viola busied herself in her cinnamon roll, ignoring the chastisement of her best friend. She grabbed her champagne, knocking down the glass, and waving over the waiter for a refill.

She knew Hannah was kidding around. Her best friend always had her back, regardless of whatever untraditional or even controversial choices Viola made for her life. Nevertheless, she knew there was some truth behind her words. Hannah wanted her friend to be happy. And happiness to her, as it was for seemingly everyone else, was finding a life partner and settling down. Finding "true love."

Viola slammed back a swig of her new mimosa as soon as the waiter sat it down. Ruby and Hannah exchanged a *look* and Ruby waved the waiter over herself.

"How about just some orange juice from now on?" She suggested. She turned back to her sister with a sympathetic smile.

"You really think it's best that I be sober when I talk about my ex?" Viola groaned and polished off the glass.

"Why *did* you break things off with Matt, anyway? You never wanted to talk about it." Ruby asked the question gently, not applying any real pressure on her sister to answer. Still, Viola could see that she really wanted to know. That she cared about what happened in her life.

"You know me, married to my cat and my career," Vi jested. "Things just got... too serious."

"Well," Hannah reached across the table and forked off another bite of cinnamon roll. She popped it into her mouth and winked at her friend, expertly diffusing the moment of awkward emotion. "I will admit that Duncan is the best kisser and cuddler I've ever met."

"Woman, you insist on woundin' me." Aaron joked, a hand to his heart.

They returned to the breakfast, the conversation shifting back to honeymoon plans and a roast of all the guests from the night before. They stayed for far too long, sending the waiters running back and forth for more bottomless mimosas.

Behind the frivolity, though, Viola's mind was fixed somewhere else. Not for the first time, she felt a bit like a disappointment. She wanted to want Matt. She had hated breaking things off with him. She had dreaded telling him how she felt, put it off for weeks before finally making the confrontation. But she hadn't been able to ignore what was lurking just beneath the surface of their relationship. She couldn't stop the conversation they'd had again and again and again, like a *Westworld* loop. In the end, Viola would stay Viola and Matt would stay Matt and she couldn't change who she was to fit what he wanted. And after all was said and done and she'd returned the ring, she had felt exactly as she did now.

Underneath the skepticism and the biting wisecracks, Viola really hoped she was wrong about love. But she just couldn't see it. With two bitterly divorced parents and her own history of unsuccessful relationships, she hadn't seen love up close and she certainly hadn't felt it for herself. After that final difficult conversation with Matt was over, had she really lost anything more than a friend with benefits?

That last, now-cold bite of cinnamon roll was starting to taste like sand in her mouth. Her friends had been joking about Hardly Committed Hardison, but if Viola wasn't around maybe they'd have their own things to say about Regrettably Single Reed.

She got up from the table and started toward the bathroom, but she stumbled over her own two feet. She collapsed into Aaron, whose face split into a grin as he winked at her.

"Whoa, nelly. Save the handsy stuff for Hardison."

Viola tried her best not to roll her eyes as she made her way back to the bathroom.

Chapter 6

"Seriously?" Viola asked as she collapsed onto her couch, running a hand through her hair as she balanced her cell phone on her shoulder. "How are you already separated? I just saw you two the other day. Sally looked happy. Although I guess that could have just been her lip filler and not a real smile..."

"It's Sandra," her father corrected her. "And it's not a separation; it's a break. A tiny one. We just need some time apart."

Viola sighed. "Let me guess: *you* need some time apart to see other women?"

"No, no." Her father cleared his throat. "Sandra just needs some time apart to *forgive* me for seeing some other women. She'll get over it and we'll be back together before Thanksgiving."

"Mhmm."

Viola was already mentally checking out of the conversation as she stood up to go rifle through her fridge. It had been weeks since Hannah's wedding, but this was the first time since that she'd spoken to her father. She tripped over Duncan, who had positioned himself by her feet to beg for treats. His little orange face looked up at her with infinite sadness as he gave a loud mew. She sighed and headed for the treat cabinet instead.

"Dad, do you think we can talk about this later? I've got a deadline coming up, and I really need to get some work done."

"Well," her father huffed. "Forgive me for trying to connect with my favorite daughter."

"I'm your only daughter," Viola said with a dry laugh. "And it's not you trying to forge a connection if I was the one who originally called to remind you about the shipping on Ruby's shower gift."

Per usual, Vi could hear Ruby's voice in her head as soon as she let the sarcasm fly. *He's trying.* Maybe she had been the one to call her dad. But he had confided in her, right? He had told her about Sandra and they'd had an actual, real conversation. He was letting her in, inviting her to venture beyond the stone wall she'd erected years before.

But even with Ruby's voice in the back of her head, it was hard for Viola to offer up her own peace in return. Dan's petition for her to return to him would go without response... at least for now.

"Alright, Viola, I get it." Her father sighed. "Do me a favor and don't bring this up when you see your stepsister? You know how fretful she gets, just like her mother used to be."

"You got it." Viola clicked off the phone.

She stepped over to her writing desk, opening the blinds to the big bay window before she sat down. The light streamed in, warming her face and relaxing her. Now wasn't the time to waste energy thinking about her father.

Viola opened her laptop and pulled up her draft. Ugh. The brief moment of relaxation disappeared near-instantly as she caught sight of her still-frustrating sequel. Sure, she'd had the recent breakthrough with Jean-Luc and his wet shirt, but the rest of the story was starting to feel simply uninspired. More and more lately, she'd been writing almost exclusively in stereotypes and boiler plate plot devices, but this was becoming a slog even for her.

A steady grinding sound began across the street. Viola stood up and crossed over to the window. The office building down the street was getting renovations, courtesy of a very heavy, very loud, very annoying excavator. She rubbed her temples, fighting back the frustration.

Her phone buzzed and she glanced at the screen. Her stomach dropped as she saw Matt's name.

It was great to see you the other day. Any chance I could buy you a coffee soon? Catch up? Monday maybe? Or Tuesday.

Viola's fingers quivered over the phone keypad. She didn't know what to say.

A new message buzzed in, taking her off guard.

Ugh, that was too much. Pretend I just texted you a *Simpsons* gif like a normal, not-obsessed person.

She smiled. Matt was as endearing and sweet as he had been the other morning. But still, the text from him had been a final straw. She could feel her insides dancing around as she considered how she'd need to reply to him soon. She needed to get away from her apartment for a moment.

Viola walked back to her laptop, removing a lounging Duncan from her keyboard to pack it up in her satchel. She slipped on her Vans, slung the bag over her shoulder, and headed for the front door. It was time for a scenery change.

She willed Jean-Luc and his dripping wet shirts from her mind as she passed by the renovations and looked for a joint with Internet access. Her usual coffee shop was out; it was too close to the excavator. She'd still be hearing the same noises all day. Ruby's house was out, too, as Scott was home working and needed the privacy.

She got far enough away in her search that she soon found herself near the Chinese restaurant from the other night. It had looked so abandoned. She remembered a little sign for free Wi-Fi. And, best of all, it meant freshly made egg rolls. Viola tucked her bag close to her body and headed the few streets over to the restaurant.

Sure enough, the space was just as empty as it was the first time she'd eaten there. Viola flagged down the same tired, greasy waitress from before as she picked out a booth and settled in.

"You ready?" The waitress asked, pulling her pad from her apron pocket and putting a hand on her hip.

"Egg rolls to start, please. Some Xiaolongbao. A Coke?"

The waitress nodded without actually writing anything down. Viola turned back to her table, retrieving her laptop from the satchel and plugging it into a socket under the booth. She opened it up, feeling the anxiety tighten in her stomach as the light came on. What was she going to do with this frustrating sequel?

"Shut up!"

Viola looked up. Brooks Hardison stood by her booth, grinning, a well-dressed brunette at his side.

"Did you dream about the egg rolls ever since we left this place, too?" She asked him, giving a dreamy smile.

"I've actually ordered takeout from here a few times since," he confessed with a smile. The brunette cleared her throat loudly, putting a well-manicured hand on her hip as she raised one delicately plucked eyebrow. "This is Ashley. Ashley, this is Reed."

"Viola Reed," she clarified, as she stuck a hand across the booth for the girl to shake. Ashley shook only the tips of her fingers, a dainty movement that seemed to indicate she would rather be doing anything else. "Well, it's good to see you again, Hardison. I'm just going to get some work done now." She gestured around the table at her small piles of character sheets, plot outlines, and various fountain pens.

"Sure, definitely." Brooks nodded, waving her off.

He led Ashley over to a table nearby, where he pulled out a chair for her. Ashley didn't sit right away, though, instead waving a hand as she disappeared to the back of the restaurant. Brooks took a seat awkwardly and pulled out his phone to play for a bit.

Viola turned back to her keyboard. The writing still wasn't coming easily because she just couldn't connect to Jean-Luc. She was caught in an endless cycle of typing out a sentence, backtracking, typing it out again. Finally, she transferred the whole thing under her "supplementary" folder and moved on to the next chapter.

"I can't be that guy who's playing on his phone at a table by himself." Brooks had slid into the booth seat across from her, making Viola jump. "Ashley said she had to go powder her nose for a minute. But she's taking so long that I'm starting to suspect she's just redoing her face entirely."

"I'm sorry," Viola said, shooting him a look before burying herself in her story once more. "I'm trying to get some work done."

"So what's your story about, anyway?" He asked, leaning over to try to catch a look at her screen.

Viola sighed. Apparently, writing several chapters simply wasn't in the cards today. "There's a French farm boy, Jean-Luc, who has to leave his true love to go to war." She explained. "He left in my last book, and in this sequel, he's finally getting back together with Marie, his sweetheart. But alas—she's already got a new boyfriend. It's all very dramatic."

"Isn't that essentially the plot to every romance ever? *Pearl Harbor?* One of the *Twilights?*"

"Ouch!" Viola winced. "One book description in and you're already comparing me to sparkly vampires. Now, if you'll excuse me—"

She gestured to her laptop, but Brooks plowed on, ignoring the hint.

"You're really into this cliché stuff, huh?" He said, settling into her booth and making himself at home. He reached across the table and took a drink from her complimentary water. Viola raised an eyebrow, but he didn't seem to think twice. "All the swooning and fainting and stuff?"

"Swooning and fainting are basically the same thing, but I'll allow it." Viola couldn't help but laugh.

"Irregardless."

At the mention of such bad grammar, Viola slapped a hand to her forehead and winced. When she opened her eyes, Brooks was winking at her. "Don't worry," he continued. "I was just kidding. So, the clichés?"

"The clichés," Viola repeated. "Aren't all love stories just a bunch of gag-worthy tropes? People eat this stuff up. It's why Hallmark and Valentine's Day exist."

Brooks took her water again and chugged the rest of it, much to Viola's chagrin. "You might be even more cynical than I thought before, Reed. What relationship wronged you so much to make you this jaded?"

"No one relationship," Viola said. "It was more like a lifetime."

She knew her face must be darkening as she thought back on her father and her mother. There was a time that they had lived out the first part of a fairy-tale themselves. She had seen the dating pictures. The honeymoon video where they sat on a white sand beach drinking sparkly cocktails.

But she could still remember the dark times, too. She could still remember the screaming matches and how she'd throw away all of her mother's beer whenever she got the chance. She could still remember the faded jean jacket and crimped blonde hair of the custody advisor that used to visit their home and monitor Viola's interactions with her parents. She could still remember meeting Ruby for the first time and thinking *Don't get too comfortable* when her father and Andrea celebrated their first anniversary together.

And, worst of all—far worse than any awkward, stilting phone calls she might have with Dan—she could remember what it was like to visit her mother for the last time before she gave up all custody and moved on with her new family.

Viola pulled her keyboard closer to her and tried to busy herself in it. Better to cut a conversation like this one off quickly, before she couldn't get any writing done—

"Ah, did some pretty boy not call you back fast enough? Heaven forbid he asked you to go Dutch at a dinner date? Gotta hate that."

Brooks was kidding around, but he still looked at her expectantly. He wasn't going to let this go any time soon. Viola sighed, rolling her eyes. Nevertheless, she felt the hot blush of her cheeks as she searched for any explanation that didn't make her sound broken and pathetic.

"Look, my parents may not have been the best example

of a healthy relationship," she started, irritated that he was pressing her.

His eyebrows raised. "And that means..." He waved her on with a flick of the wrist.

"It means," she started, still a little hesitant. "That growing up was really hard with two parents who were never happy together or with me. Love was never really a part of the equation."

"And so the clichés are—"

"Maybe it's just easier to write in clichés than to try and paint a picture of the truth as it really is," she snapped, trying to rush the conversation along. "Maybe it gives me some sense of control, okay?" She couldn't help but feel defensive; this was touching on some sensitive areas that she didn't want to even think about right now.

Brooks looked at her seriously, his eyes crinkling in the corners as he thought. Finally, he put out a palm. "You're welcome for the therapy breakthrough, Reed; that'll be fifty bucks." He grinned.

Viola rolled her eyes. But she couldn't help it—she smiled back.

"Your date is back from the bathroom," she said. "Don't order anything too steamy or that new layer of makeup she just put on might melt off into your egg rolls."

"Noted." Brooks smiled and stood back up, knocking his knuckles against the table a few times. He gave Viola a little wave before joining Ashley at his table.

Viola turned back to her laptop, rolling back her shoulders and popping her neck. Jean-Luc, hello again. She threw her mind back into the novel, trying her best to ignore the sounds of the restaurant kitchen and Brooks' conversation with his date and immerse herself in French farm territory.

Once again, though, Jean-Luc failed to come to life for her. Instead of focusing on him and Marie, Viola found herself thinking about another young man. One she could swear was still watching her from the corner of his eye.

CHAPTER 7

AUTUMN

"Trite?"

Viola rolled her eyes as she paced around her apartment living room. She figured she must be the only person alive still in possession of a landline, and the long cord curled in a twisted trail behind her now as she spoke on the phone with her agent.

"Francine, *everything* I do is trite. Trite sells. Trite paid for your vacation to the Bahamas last month."

She could hear the puff of cigarette smoke as Francine blew out a tired gust. "I'm not sure what else to call it, Viola. I could swear that I've read your sequel before in at least half a dozen books in my slush pile. It's been done."

Viola collapsed onto her couch, squinting her eyes shut as she tried to maintain her composure. "It's *all* been done. Everything I write is essentially a variation on something else that I've already written. Jean-Luc is Mark is Benoit is Noah. They're all the same because that's what readers want."

"Well, it's not what these readers want." Francine's signature overlong red nails *tap-tapped* on a keyboard as she spoke. *Great.* Viola's agent wasn't even invested in this conversation enough to stop sending her emails. "At least a quarter of your beta readers surveyed said that they didn't even make it to the end of your story. You've been at this for years; maybe it's time to shake things up."

Duncan hopped into Viola's lap, purring loudly and looking up at her with begging eyes. She scooped him up and placed him on his own cushion, getting back to her feet to pace once more. Her sequel was still pulled up on her laptop as she walked by. She couldn't begin to understand. She was the best at what she did. Her agent knew that, her readers knew that, and her sales proved it beyond all doubt. Why would she change?

"And how would you suggest that I shake things up?" she asked.

"Give me something more real," Francine suggested, taking another puff from the unseen cigarette. "Maybe something personal."

"Personal," Viola snorted. "Fran, come on. Couldn't you just suggest something more feasible for me to do with my time, like base jumping off the Eiffel Tower or robbing the Smithsonian?"

Viola could hear the sounds of a busy street and knew that Francine had left her office for lunch. She was losing her window of opportunity to help her agent to see her side of things.

"If you don't have something personal, go find some inspiration," Francine suggested, sounding harried. "You're young and beautiful: seduce a neighbor, call up an ex-boyfriend, flirt with a stranger!"

Viola could feel a headache coming on fast. Her eyes darted to the cabinet where she kept her wine. She'd already been feeling so stressed with her sequel deadline and now, what? Francine just expected her to scrap it and write something completely new? And worse—she thought that it would be a good idea for Viola to get inspired for the text by getting her hands on some real-world romance? Her agent obviously wasn't privy to the pathetic details of her dating life.

"Alright, alright." Viola finally conceded. "I'll try to come up with some grand idea to hunt down some inspiration."

"Excellent, honey. Get me a new draft to read in four months?"

"*Four months?*"

The headache had shifted from irritating pressure into needling pain just above her brow. Viola's annoyance had evolved into a full-on panic.

"Francine, come on. You're asking for a whole new book made from scratch!"

"I've had years to become familiar with your production rate, Viola. You push more quantity than any of my other writers."

"You're insane."

"And that's why you keep me around, darling." Francine laughed, a husky sound which quickly turned into a hacking cough. "We'll touch base soon."

"But I—"

"Toodle-oo!"

Viola sat, frozen, on her couch, the phone still pressed up against her ear. She didn't even know how to begin to write something new.

Finally, she got up. Duncan slid off her lap, complaining with a loud mew in her direction before finding a comfortable new spot on the windowsill. Viola paced, nervously twisting the cord of her landline around and around and around her finger.

When it came to creative wells to draw from, she knew that her life might as well be the driest desert. Jeez, the last time she had even watched a rom-com was when she had accidentally caught part of *A Walk to Remember* on TV and started out a live tweet to roast the dialogue.

Still... she knew that she was in trouble if she didn't at least attempt to change. Francine wasn't the kind of agent to mess with something that worked for her. She'd been rocking the same haircut and shoulder pads since before Vi had even met her. For her to come to her now about changing, the situation had to be serious. Viola knew that she had to do something drastic and do it fast.

Viola's eyes darted to her little writing desk. The drawer was half-open, and she could see the Whitman collection just peeking out, mocking her. Walt would never be accused of writing something trite. He was a real author. He was a Romantic sure, but as in the Romantic literary movement, not the kiss-me-on-your-balcony, poison-yourself-for-me kind of way. He was a *real* author.

Viola paused in her pacing as she passed by her junk drawer. It was still littered with invitations for the start of wedding season, sticking out at odd angles and fighting for limited space. For the past few weeks, she had mostly tried to ignore these invitations, figuring that she would send a gift card and call things a day. Now, though, she pulled the drawer all the way open and plucked one up, with a date stamped in bold for that weekend.

Caitlin Cross to marry Hunter Smith. Ruby would be at this one with Scott. It was obviously too late to RSVP, but Caitlin was an old roommate from the sorority so maybe if she texted...

Viola swallowed down her pride and marched off to her bedroom, throwing open the doors of her closet to find the cocktail dress she'd worn at Hannah's wedding. It was in a crumpled heap on her floor, one strap still hooked together where Viola had drunkenly tried to remove it in the dark before collapsing on to her bed that night. She picked it up gingerly, examining the damage. Ugh. Guess she'd have to get the number for that dry cleaner from Ruby after all.

Chapter 8

Viola figured that Caitlin and Hunter must have known every wealthy person in the tri-state area. Their wedding was glitz and glam, packed to the brim with men in tuxedos and women dripping with pearls. Viola's cheeks had worn a permanent shade of red through the whole ceremony as she tried to hide her shabby second-hand cocktail dress under Scott's borrowed suit jacket. It was clear to her now that Caitlin's last-minute acceptance of her RSVP had been a charitable act.

Despite her appearance, though, Viola had devoted herself to her task at hand. As her tender-hearted sister was getting teary-eyed during the vows, Viola was jotting notes in her phone and improving upon what the couple had written for each other. *Come on, Francine*, she thought. Wasn't "I vow to love you until my dying breath" pretty trite, too?

From under a hymn book, she'd texted Matt about her dilemma. They'd chatted off and on since his message the other day, none of it compelling her to make any firm plans to go out with him, but every message leaving her with a sense of wistfulness.

He had written back to her that Caitlin and Hunter should have vowed to love each other until Caitlin got too old or Hunter got too much of a beer gut. Viola couldn't help but chuckle at that.

"Come up with anything good?" Scott asked her as the guests started to file out of the chapel and into the reception hall next door.

"I liked that Caitlin sang for Hunter," Ruby piped up. "Not that I'm going to do that at our ceremony." She blushed.

"Come on, baby, just hit me with one verse of 'Everything I Do.'" Scott grinned.

Viola groaned. A waiter passed by carrying a tray of champagne, and she flagged him down to steal a glass. The drink went down smooth and cold. "I swear I've written all this before," she said. "I'm just not sure what Francine expects of me."

"Lucky for you, Scott and I already thought of another real-world experience that might help you out." Ruby cleared her throat and took Vi's half-drained glass to quickly dispose of it. She had a twinkle in her eye as she stood on her tiptoes, waving at a gentleman in the distance. "Andrew! Over here!"

The man turned, revealing a broad smile full of sparkling white teeth. He was tall, dark, and handsome, for sure, with rich chocolate dimples that sent Viola's stomach into little flips. Still, it wasn't enough to overcome her irritation. The weak smile she offered him came out feeling more like a grimace.

"Ruby! Scott!" Andrew leaned in to kiss Vi's sister on the cheek before clapping his friend on the back.

"Viola, Andrew is an old housemate of mine." Scott explained. "He works as a copywriter out in Nashville." Scott's eyebrows waggled with emphasis on the last line, and it was clear to Viola that her future brother-in-law thought that a mutual love for the written word—apparently any word at all—was enough to forge a romantic connection.

"It's a pleasure to meet you." Andrew offered his hand for her to shake.

"You as well," she said, taking it for a cursory sweaty shake. "I'm so sorry; has anyone seen the waiter running around here with champagne? I've already gone through my glass."

"I wish," Andrew laughed. "I needed something to get me through that ceremony. I mean, how many times can I watch a bride sing off-key for her new husband?"

Viola felt her sister elbow her. Ruby was grinning, surely convinced that she'd finally broken through with this new match.

Viola knew that she probably ought to stick around and give Andrew a chance. Even if it wasn't a love connection, he could be her next great hero, right?

Maybe he had a dark side. No, wait. That was a romance trope. *A tragic past?* That had been a done a million times before, too. Was there any backstory for Andrew that *hadn't* already been written into a million Hallmark movies? Her efforts began to feel pointless. Even if Andrew turned out to be the most perfect human since Gandhi, he would still be a useless, boring, predictable stock character that was of no use to her know. Viola could feel the panic setting back in. She itched to fall back on old habits and get away.

"I think I'm going to make a run for the bar," she announced.

Ruby leaned over to whisper in her ear. "Come on, Vi,

wasn't it your main man Walt Whitman who said to 'be curious, not judgmental'?"

"How dare you try and use a literary genius against me?" Viola muttered back.

"Andrew can go with you?" Scott offered on his friend's behalf.

"I'm good, I'm good." She waved them off. "Catch up, have some fun."

Viola turned and darted off through the crowd before Scott or Ruby could voice more objections. She almost felt bad for bailing on their carefully laid plan. Almost.

On her way to the bar, she passed plenty more tropes ripped straight from the pages of her novels. Old lovers reconnected on the dance floor, swaying and hugging each other close as they reminisced about their own weddings. Young men tapped young women on the shoulder, each with their own witty prepared pick-up line. Worst of all, Viola felt the stab of sympathy as she spotted awkward, single girls like her hovering around the fringes of the crowd, desperately hoping for a little company.

When she reached the bar, she found that she wasn't the only person in want of a drink after all that romantic bliss. She waved a pitiful hand, knowing already that the bartender was never going to see her through all the silk and linen-clad guests waving fifties in his direction. She huffed a little, crossing her arms.

"You're kidding me." A familiar voice came from behind her.

Viola turned. Brooks stood before her, a blond draped on each of his arms. The women were average, maybe even a little plain, but Brooks was beaming at his big catch. "Ladies, I'm so sorry to cut this short, but it seems that I've run into an old friend. You can go. Make some more friends while you're gone to bring back to me."

The girls giggled, and one of them swatted him on the arm. "You're simply terrible, Mr. Hardison," she said, a French accent barely making itself known. She winked at Viola. "Take care of this one, he's something else." They waggled their fingers at him before walking off arm in arm toward the dance floor.

It took all of Viola's energy not to roll her eyes. Yeah, he really was something else. But maybe not the emotionally intelligent charmer these girls seemed to believe that he was.

Brooks sidled up at the bar next to Viola, one eyebrow raised. "I didn't expect to see the world's greatest cynic at another wedding so soon. I thought you only attended the mandatory stuff and left the rest of us heathens to romance by ourselves."

"Usually that's the case," she agreed. Viola waved her arm at the bartender again. He didn't bat an eye in her direction. "Apparently, my novels have stopped feeling 'real' lately. I'm here on assignment by my agent to find some new ideas. Besides, Caitlin is another sorority sister."

"Hunter was a brother in my fraternity," Brooks noted with a nod of his head. "It seems there's something in the water making everyone we went to school with fall in love and pop out babies all at the same time. So what are we drinking that's prevented us from doing the same?"

"Lots and lots of champagne," Viola said, waggling her empty glass.

Brooks raised his arm and snapped his fingers at the bartender who still didn't see them.

"So how'd they get you to come to this one?" Viola asked him.

"Apparently perfect, single Emily was an Atlanta Hawks dancer after college and her favorite drink is tequila. She was supposed to be seated next to me and it sounded too enticing to turn down. You seen any Emilys tonight?"

Viola laughed and shook her head. Brooks glanced back up at the bar again. When the bartender didn't so much as turn in their direction, he pushed himself up onto the counter and snagged a bottle of something dark and red before passing it to Viola. He slapped a bill down by the register. Viola gasped at his audacity, but a thrill shot through her. This was something new.

"What?" He shrugged as she laughed at him. "I paid for it. Come join me for a minute, Reed."

He put a hand on the small of her back, guiding her through the crowd to an empty table. She got a funny feeling as his fingertips brushed her skin, something that she didn't quite have the right words to describe. A spasm? Did he accidentally static shock her? Even as a writer, descriptors were really failing her. Whatever it was, she opted to shimmy away and keep her distance.

They sat down, with Brooks pulling the bottle of wine toward him to uncork it with a house key. He handed it to Viola. "Ladies first."

She held it in both hands and knocked down a massive swig. After she finished swallowing, she wiped at her mouth with the back of her hand, feeling a little embarrassed at the liquid that had escaped from the corners of her mouth.

Brooks smirked. "Someone looks like they needed that tonight."

"You have no idea," she groaned. "I'm at a total loss. I'm uninspired."

"Lucky for you, I've been dying to pitch you some ideas since we spoke last. I'm thinking seriously about giving everything up to pursue my own career in romance writing." Brooks leaned back, draping his arm over the seat next to him.

She collapsed onto the table, arms splayed out. She lifted two fingers to wave at him. "Lay 'em on me," she muttered into the tablecloth.

"Okay, picture this: two teenagers from rival families meet and fall in love."

"That's *Romeo and Juliet*."

"Okay, picture this: it's *Breaking Bad*, but the two drug dealers decide that they want to be a couple by the of the story."

"Hardison, I swear—"

"Okay, picture *this*: two people have an epic love story that spans time and space, but in the end, it actually turns out to be the story of your relationship with your cat and all your readers realized that they've been tricked into reading something really sad and pathetic."

"That could sell." Viola sat up, laughing.

"Right?" Brooks smiled and thought for a moment as he pulled the bottle toward himself and took his own drink. Finally, he smacked both hands down on the table, coming to a firm decision. "I've got it. You should come with me to my parent's anniversary party!"

Viola snorted. "I'm sorry?"

"Seriously," he explained. "They've been married for, like, forty years or something. It's going to be huge. Plenty of romance and inspiration. You'll be bursting at the seams with ideas for the next *Nights in Rodanthe*."

She laughed and took the bottle back. "I didn't know people really stayed married for forty years anymore. Shouldn't that be illegal? Isn't there an increased risk that they'll poison each other's Metamucil or something?"

Brooks shrugged and smiled. "Who knows, maybe this party will be the tipping point. I'll hide all the cake-cutting knives beforehand as a general precaution. At the very least, you'll have a violent new anecdote for one of your stories."

"Alright," Viola finally agreed. "That might actually sound like... fun." She smiled and took another swig of wine.

"It's 'not a date.'" Brooks grinned.

Chapter 9

"So it's basically going to be like a second wedding?"

"Yeah," Brooks answered, nodding his head. "Basic anniversary meets vow renewal meets excuse for all our neighbors to shower them in gifts. Hence, the registry."

The pair had found themselves in a Williams-Sonoma on a Saturday morning, with Viola feeling completely lost in a crowd of amateur chefs and well-to-do soccer moms. She and Brooks had been texting on and off since the last wedding, making plans for his parents' anniversary party and sending roasts of their fellow wedding guests. In fact, they'd been talking so much that when Brooks popped the idea of shopping on her, Viola hadn't stopped to think things through and said yes. So here she was, two strangers' anniversary registry pulled up on her phone, with absolutely no idea what the difference was between sauté pan and a saucepan.

"I definitely think you invited the wrong person to come with you." She shook her head, picking up something heavy and cast-iron and inspecting it through squinted eyes. "The closest I've come to any pots and pans is the open-air kitchen at my favorite takeout place."

"Ooh, do you think we could call them for a recommendation on what to buy?" Brooks asked.

Viola put a hand in her bag to retrieve her phone. "Great idea! I've got their number on speed dial."

"Jeez, Reed, I was kidding." Brooks laughed. His dark eyes crinkled happily in the corners. It made him look mature and content. All offense that might have been taken over the joke was instantly banished.

"Okay, so maybe I'll opt for something non-culinary." Viola scanned the list once more. "Your parents registered for the complete boxed set of *Home Improvement*? A membership to Ben and Jerry's flavor of the month club?"

"They've been married for a while. They know what they want." Brooks shrugged.

"Sexopoly: The Board Game for All Your Bedroom Needs?"

Brooks leapt over and tried to snatch back the registry list, his cheeks blossoming a bright red. Viola laughed and pulled the paper to her chest. "Kidding," she assured him with a wink.

"Well, we're already in Williams-Sonoma so we might as well get them something practical." He said, returning to business as the pink on his face subsided a little. "Thankfully, one of us knows what appliances properly belong in a home. We'll get them a crepe pan; my dad would love a new one. Makes a killer chicken mushroom crepe for breakfast."

Brooks scooped up what they needed from off a shelf and headed for checkout. Viola reached into her pocket to produce her wallet, but he waved her off. "I've got this."

Viola stood off to the side, ruminating while Brooks made his rather expensive purchase. She didn't like the idea of her not contributing toward the gift for his parents. She knew how these things went: first you're hanging out, then he's paying for you, maybe you get a little too drunk at the next wedding reception where you kiss each other, and *wham, bam, thank you ma'am*. You're full-blown dating.

Okay, okay... she knew that the logic of it all sounded more than a little juvenile. But still, she'd written enough of these enemy-turned-lover romances in her novels to know how these things went. She wasn't about to let this turn into a relationship. The devil was in the details.

She grabbed Brooks' arm as he stepped away from the register. "I've got lunch."

"Okay," he shrugged, clearly not as hung up as Viola was.

They left Williams-Sonoma, walking through the mall back to the food court. Brooks pointed out a Chinese restaurant, and they jumped into line.

"I think this might start to become our thing," he cracked.

Viola's face flushed. She wanted to change the subject. "So how'd you know all about those pots and pans and stuff?"

"I *am* more than a pretty face, ya know." He chastised her with a smile. "'That stuff' is actually my favorite way to relax. I make some killer pork dumplings if you ever want to come over."

They shuffled down the line, finally arriving at the register. Viola pulled out her wallet and paid as they continued to talk.

"But how did you learn to cook?" She asked. "I found out the hard way that I basically know the bare minimum to survive a pandemic."

A familiar, dark flash waved across Brooks' face as he

took his tray and began to find a table. "Old girlfriend," he answered. "If Asian food is my thing with you, then food in general was kind of my thing with her. She taught me all the basics."

"Brooks Hardison actually committed to someone long enough to pick up a life skill?" Viola raised an eyebrow at him as she pulled out a chair and sat down. "Color me shocked."

"I know, I know." He said, looking more withdrawn than she had ever seen.

Brooks quickly shoved a bite of food in his mouth, a diversion tactic that Viola knew well. She picked up her own chopsticks and prodded at an egg roll, wondering what a girl who might date Hardly Committed Hardison would even be like. Had he had other serious girlfriends before? She felt like she was tapping into a whole new layer of Brooks that she hadn't seen yet.

He chewed in silence, clearly trying to leave the conversation behind. But Viola couldn't let it go.

"How long were you guys together?" She asked.

"Can we not do this?" Brooks asked. "I don't poke at you about your ex."

Viola shrugged. "I don't mind. Maybe we could both ask and answer questions? Go tit for tat?"

Brooks put down his chopsticks, crossed his arms, and sat back to look at her. The little line between his eyebrows had grown deep, but she could see the barest hint of a smile hiding in the corner of his mouth. "Alright. What was his name?"

"Matt," she answered.

"Matt," Brooks repeated, looking like he had a sour taste in his mouth. "Did you really have to date someone so basic, Reed? There are way cooler names out there."

"Like Brooks?" She teased. "Mhmm. Sure." She cleared her throat, feeling her cheeks turn their own shade of pink. That last line was a little too close to flirting. She straightened up. "What was your ex's name?"

"Chelsea."

"Come on!" Viola threw up her hands in mock-protest. She couldn't help it: she *had* to tease him a little bit. "You can't come at me when you dated someone with such a basic white girl name! Was her middle name Marie? Nicole, maybe?"

"No, definitely not!" He burst into laughter.

"Alright," Viola sat back in her own seat, thinking. "How did you meet?"

"High school sweethearts," Brooks answered.

"You were *not*." She shook her head. "I'm a romance novelist, dipstick. Consequently, I know that the percentage of high school sweethearts who make it past graduation are—"

"Not good, I know," he said. "Hey, there's a reason we didn't make it past college graduation down the road. But I took Chelsea to high school prom and everything, I swear. I think we both know that I can be quite charming in a tie and boutonniere. What about you and Matt?"

"Blind date," Viola admitted with a shrug. "My sister and best friend had been trying to set me up for years and I finally relented. I guess I didn't have the willpower after such an ordeal to ever tell Matt to get lost and go home."

"Okay, my turn for a new question." Brooks ran a hand through the slight stubble that had grown out on his chin. Finally, he propped his elbows up on the table and eyeballed Viola. "Tell me what you found most attractive about Matt."

"Gosh, Hardison." Viola rolled her eyes.

Despite her distaste for Brooks' question, though, the obvious answers came to her mind quickly. Matt was classically good-looking. Tall. Toned. A jawline to kill. But that wasn't what had kept her hanging out with him, was it? It wasn't what had driven her to allow a small place in her life for him. To open up her home. Her heart.

"He worked to become my friend first," she said finally.

"Not a bad answer," Brooks said solemnly. "But now I'm going to look like an imbecile."

"Why? What did you find most attractive about Chelsea?"

He looked up at Viola, wide-eyed and innocent. "Her butt."

Viola burst into laughter. The awkwardness of opening up about her breakup melted away.

"Alright," she said. "My turn now. Why did you break up?"

In a flash, the mood changed. It was Brooks' turn to look uncomfortable now; his playfulness and gentility hardened as quickly as it had come on. His eyes were dark as he busied himself with his food once more. "I think this game might have run its course."

"Come on," Viola started. "You don't have to give me the play-by-play. I've basically already told you my own reason. Matt wanted me to be someone that I wasn't."

Viola had to take a deep breath here. It was surprisingly hard talking about the end of her relationship with Matt. "I couldn't ... I *wouldn't* change who I was for someone else. Even if it was for someone that maybe I could love."

"Okay," Brooks nodded, finally looking up at her. "Then I guess you could say that our breakups weren't that different. Chelsea wished that I was someone else, too. It's ancient history."

Viola nodded understandingly, and they turned back to their plates in silence. For someone who thrived on the quiet and solitude of her no-roommate apartment and work-from-home career, she couldn't swallow down her growing sense of unease. She had jokingly pegged Brooks as the playboy with a dark past, sure, but she hadn't expected him to have had that intense of a breakup. She hadn't even expected him to have ever been in a committed relationship at all. She wished he would speak now, say anything. Call her "Reed" again and make fun of her lack of adult skills. Anything to leave this awkwardness behind.

She stood up then, her chair squealing as it pushed out behind her. "I've got to tell you, Hardison, I don't feel comfortable with you paying for my part of your parents' gift. I think we should head across the street to the Target and pick out a crock pot. That's unique, right?"

Brooks put a hand to his forehead, rolling his eyes. "Honestly, Reed. I don't know how you survive as a func-tioning member of society. They've had four crock pots sitting in our kitchen closet since their first wedding forty years ago. Maybe you could get them some new coasters? Or there's a set of wind chimes my mom has had her eye on for ages..."

His voice faded off as he stood up from the table and headed off to lead her out of the food court. Viola lingered behind for a moment, smiling to herself relieved. Though there was a bit of a rough patch, it felt good to help him return to his normal self.

Chapter 10

Seeing Brooks Hardison in barbecue attire felt a lot like seeing a dog walk on its hind legs. They had talked on and off all morning via text, but his face and body were hidden behind his cell phone screen. The only pictures Viola had in her mind were of Brooks in his black tux, grinning like a doofus at his latest wedding date, or at the mall, looking suave and charming in what he had pretentiously called his "going out jeans" and an expensive polo. She had thought he lived for designer clothing. Even his Bitmoji was wearing a tie. Seeing him now was nothing short of a shock.

Viola shook her head as he held his car door open for her, gesturing for her to get inside. "Tell me you don't wear those flip-flops to gatherings outside of your family."

Brooks blinked. "What?"

"Your toes are so white. I think I'm losing vision from the reflection of the sun."

He pretended to shove her in like a cop with an arrested criminal. "Into the car, Reed. No making fun of the driver."

"Seriously?" She teased. "You're lucky you wear those

shiny black Oxfords when you pick up women. There's no way any of them would go home with you if they knew what your feet looked like beforehand."

He turned on the car, suppressing a smile. Viola continued to take in his outfit. "And are those cargo shorts?" She asked, incredulous. "Why do you need so many pockets?"

The drive from her apartment to Brooks' parents' house was short and sweet. Whereas Viola lived in the city proper, they lived in the suburbs just off the edge of town in a row of picket fences and manicured lawns and tiny dogs that yipped when the Suburban drove by.

She hadn't grown up too far from there herself. The house she and her father had lived in with Ruby and Andrea could only be maybe ten minutes out. She remembered fueling up at a gas station they passed, attending fifth grade at an elementary school tucked away by a brightly colored playground, shopping for snacks at a slightly rundown grocery store.

Viola wondered if she had ever met Brooks before wedding season. If they had run into each other as children right here in the neighborhood. It was an unexpected thought that left her stomach feeling oddly unsettled.

"Here we are," Brooks pronounced, parking his car in the drive of a modest two-story.

The home was decked to the nines and bursting with people. Balloons hung on the mailbox, bunched together in so many numbers that they looked as though they might accidentally pop one another. Multi-colored streamers adorned the doorway, as did a sign that read "Congratulations, Kathy and Wayne!" The backyard fence gaped open, and Viola could spot an older man at a barbecue wearing a funny apron and showing off his burger-flipping skills. Everyone here looked happy.

As they got out of the car, a little boy with a wild mess of blonde curls came streaking through the lawn toward them. He grabbed Brooks around the knees and buried his face into his cargo shorts.

"Wyatt!" Brooks scooped him up and hugged him close.

"Bobo!" The boy gave Brooks an Eskimo kiss, giggling at the tickling touch. But when he spotted Viola, he stopped his play to bashfully hide his face in Brooks' shirt collar.

"You gonna introduce me, Bobo?" Viola asked with a smile.

"Reed, this is my nephew, Wyatt. He gets his good looks from me."

Viola dropped to her knees and raised her hand for a high-five. Finally cracking into a smile, Wyatt smacked her hand and then reached over to give her a tight hug around the neck. Viola blushed.

"What are you, like, twelve?" She joked with him as he pulled away.

"Three and a quarter," he answered very seriously. "I have a dog named Milo."

"That is very cool," Viola answered the non sequitur solemnly. "I have a cat named Duncan."

Wyatt giggled into his hands and then dashed off, back through the open fence door. Brooks offered Viola a hand, and she got up from the ground, brushing the dirt from her knees.

"Bobo, huh?"

"Shut up." He grinned. "Brooks is a hard name for a kid to say so we had to come up with something."

The pair made their way across the lawn toward the

fence. They blended in with the crowd of people as Brooks found an ice cooler and produced two frosty sodas. Viola cracked hers open and took a drink.

"I've gotta say, I never would have pegged you as a kid guy," she said.

"It's a part of my multi-faceted brand," he joked. "But seriously, I really love kids. I want, like, eight."

"*Eight*?"

"Hey," Brooks threw up his hands. "There's a reason I cast a wide net with the ladies. Gotta find my Mama Duggar out there."

She chuckled. "Good luck, dude."

"I know, I know," Brooks shook his head, hands in the air. "But I really do love kids. Even before Wyatt came along, it's the one thing I can always remember wanting. They make toddler-sized suits and ties, right?"

Brooks' tone was light, but his eyes looked vacant and far away. She wanted to push for more, but suddenly felt a little silly and embarrassed.

Viola smiled at him. "You continue to surprise me, Hardison."

"I'll take that as a compliment, Reed." He smiled back.

They were interrupted by the feeling of a touch on both of their shoulders. They turned. Before them stood a short, plump brunette woman, beaming and bouncing on her heels. She grasped Viola by the elbows and spoke directly to her.

"You must be Miss Reed!" She proclaimed. "We're so glad you could make it out to our little party!"

Viola liked her instantly. "Mrs. Hardison?"

"Call me Kathy, dear." Kathy smiled again and pulled her son close to her side, fidgeting with his hair. Brooks squirmed like a child, but his mother persisted until she finally got his curls the way that she liked them. She turned once more to Viola. "Brooks hasn't brought a girl out to see us in so long. We worried he might have joined the priesthood." She giggled. The sound was soft and bubbly. "How long has it been, love? Since Chelsea—"

"—And *that's* enough life story," Brooks said definitively, making a comical show of hugging his mother tight to silence her. Kathy smiled warmly, taking it in jest.

"Uh, she's exaggerating, by the way," Brooks muttered in Viola's ear as his mother waved across the crowd at a friend. "I mean, I haven't brought any girls home since Chelsea, but you're not, like, a *girl* girl. You're my Viola. I mean, you're Viola. You're—"

"I feel like there was an insult buried somewhere in between all that stammering and pretending like you're too macho to have ever had your heart broken?"

She grinned at Brooks and elbowed him in the ribs. He turned red at the tips of his ears, and she couldn't help but notice how his eyes darted off and away. Maybe teasing him about Chelsea was somewhere Vi shouldn't take their friendship. She wished she could take back the jab.

Kathy was turning back to the friends. She gestured wildly. "You're just in time for the good stuff," she told Viola. "We're about to cut the cake. Strawberry shortcake!"

A young woman appeared behind Kathy with Wyatt placed firmly on her hip. Viola was surprised to see that she looked exactly like Brooks, right down to the strong, broad nose. She was beautiful, though, tall and thin and confident in a way one rarely sees. She smiled and extended a hand to Viola. "I hear that Wyatt introduced himself but didn't bother to come grab his old mom. I'm Molly, Brooks' older sister."

Viola shook her hand. She felt an unexpected pain in her chest. Brooks had a good family. The dad at the barbecue. The doting mother. The sister with the adorable son. *Was she feeling jealous?*

"Has Mom had the chance to embarrass Brooks yet?" Molly asked with a wink. "I had to come over and make sure you heard the story about when he tried to steal our parents' car back in middle school."

Brooks swooped in front of his sister, arms out to block her from view. "Ignore her; she's always been desperate for attention. Classic first child syndrome."

Molly's head popped over his shoulder. "The dope stalled it at the end of the driveway and blocked the middle of our street!" She cackled, tears in her eyes. "Oh man, it was so good..."

Brooks' ears were turning red. "Um, didn't we have a conversation last time I brought friends over about putting a memorandum on embarrassing childhood stories, naked baby pictures, and all that?"

He swatted at his sister. Molly was still laughing though, happy tears in the corners of her eyes.

Kathy held out her arms for Wyatt to come to her, which he did happily. Molly waved in Viola's direction before heading back to the crowd of guests, still laughing at her anecdote about Brooks.

Kathy touched Viola's shoulder. "You'll have to come and see me again before you go. We've heard so much about you."

The red was spreading from Brooks' ears to the rest of his face. He stepped forward, offering his arm to Viola. "Wanna find a seat for the cake cutting?"

He led her away and they settled near the back fence. The crowd began to quiet down as a family friend produced the cake from her kitchen, a creamy dream of pink frosting and delicate rosebuds. Brooks' father, Wayne, tall and stately looking, joined Kathy at the center of the lawn, two glasses of champagne at the ready.

Wayne set the drinks down and pulled his bride close, leaning forward to kiss her gently on the forehead. He toasted her, telling funny stories of early marriage and serious tales of the trials they had endured together. When he was done, he stood behind her, stooping to hold Kathy's arms in place as they cut their anniversary cake.

In one jarring moment, Viola felt it: that thing that her agent had been trying to get her to pin down. Real love. It was right here, in front of her. The way that Kathy and Wayne looked at each other, touched each other, talked about each other. Even after all this time, they clung to each other like newlyweds. Viola's stomach did a little flip.

She started to lean over to Brooks, to whisper to him that she was grateful that he brought her to the party. She stopped short, though, catching sight of him watching his parents. He had a small smile still tugging up the corner of his mouth.

She was surprised at how handsome he looked then. Stripped of the fancy designer clothes, his appearance was still rather charming. His hair had curled up in the humid morning air, extending into little twisting wisps behind his ears. His dark eyes sparkled in the brilliant sun. He looked happy, relaxed. Present.

Viola was suddenly very aware of how hot and humid it had gotten outside. She pulled her hair up and into a pony-tail away from the heat of her collar. She felt a buzz in her pocket. Brooks' gaze on the cake cutting broke as she scrambled to retrieve her phone.

"All good?" He asked her quietly.

"Sorry," she whispered back.

She pulled the phone from her pocket, taking a quick peek to make sure it wasn't Ruby needing something or Francine checking in on her deadline. Her screen flashed with an incoming text: *MATT*.

Viola slipped the phone back into her pocket. She felt it there, though, buzzing again a moment later. Finally, she pulled it out, hiding it in her lap as she checked the message.

There's a cat who won't leave my front door. Made me think of my favorite cat lady.

And then, the second message:

Oh God. I hope that wasn't weird.

She chuckled under her breath.

Not weird. She wrote back. *It's always been my dream for people to think "Viola" when they think "cats."*

"Everything okay?" Brooks checked in again.

Viola clicked off the screen and shoved the phone back into her pocket. She smiled at him. "Totally." She used her phone to fan herself, desperate for any relief from this pressing heat.

The cake-cutting and toasts went on. Viola laughed at all the right parts and clapped when it was necessary. But her mind had slipped away somewhere else. Seemed like Brooks wasn't the only one with something heavy on his mind.

She was pulled back to the real world when the guests began to stand, clapping as the happy couple shared an anniversary kiss. Wayne scooped up his bride, holding her up like a prize. Kathy's face turned bright red as she struggled to keep her shirt pulled down and her updo in place, but she was grinning happily through it all.

"Well?" Brooks asked her afterward, his face expectant. "What's the verdict?"

"I have to give it to you," Viola said. "I've been to a lot of weddings and I've written about even more, but this party was almost enough to reinvent the concept of romance for me. Your parents look truly in love."

Brooks smiled at her, clearly proud. Viola could feel how flushed her cheeks were then and hoped that she didn't look as flustered and swept up as she felt. She was surprised at how much the party had really gotten to her. She stood up, pointing her thumb at the house.

"Is there maybe some water I can grab inside?"

"I'll show you the kitchen," he volunteered.

Brooks grabbed her hand and led her through the crowd toward the house. Instinct told her to pull back. Walk on her own. She couldn't say what made her hold on to his hand in return, but as they walked together, Viola felt that now-familiar rush of dizziness. They stopped frequently with Brooks being flagged down by old friends and neighbors who all had something nice to say about him and his parents. Finally, though, they made it to a white-trimmed screen door and slipped inside.

The kitchen was old school Georgian with faded white cabinetry, trim yellow curtains, and an oversized sign that read "Bless this Mess." Viola could see where the Hardisons had marked Brooks' and Molly's heights on the doorframe that led to a laundry room. Much like with seeing him in street clothes, it felt odd to picture Brooks as a child muddying up the kitchen tile or leaving his homework on the counter.

She could feel that flustered feeling picking up again, and a single bead of sweat dropped down from her ponytail onto the nape of her neck. "That water?" She reminded him.

"Patience, grasshopper." Brooks reached up and grabbed a glass from a cabinet, filling it at the fridge.

He handed it back to her, and their fingers brushed. Viola looked up at him then, surprised to find that he was watching her face and not their hands. His gaze searched hers. She felt a stirring in her chest, something soft and fluttering. The heat at the back of her neck flamed out to the rest of her body, sending sparking tingles through her fingers and toes.

Viola quickly trained her eyes on the kitchen rug, taking a swallow and then holding the icy glass to her forehead.

Physical touch, she reminded herself. Physical touch tricks the brain into creating a sense of intimacy. Just think about those long white toes in flip-flops, she reminded herself. She shivered. *That* image wouldn't be leaving her head anytime soon.

"We ought to get back," she said to him. "I don't want to miss a minute of this. It's great inspo for my book."

Brooks cleared his throat, taking a small step away toward the door. "Of course," he said, gesturing his hand for her to go first.

She started toward the exit. "It must be my day for romance-y stuff," Viola started, her voice a little halting and hesitant. "You wouldn't believe who texted me just now. Matt!"

Brooks eyes widened. They stepped back into the sunlight. The soft buzz of barbeque conversation helped Viola to ease back into a sense of normalcy.

"Wow," Brooks commented. "So are you guys... like, back together or something?"

"Um, I don't know," she answered. She let some space grow between them as she led the way through the crowd back to their seats. "I mean, he's a great guy, right? Probably a good fit for me? I think I ought to give him a fair shot."

"Sure." Brooks agreed.

For a moment, Viola wanted to look back to where he followed her through the backyard. She wanted to see his face, see what he felt behind that carefully nonchalant "sure." But she pressed forward, willing herself to stare ahead.

Chapter 11

"My inbox is empty, Viola. Keep this up and you're going to start making me think that I'm accidentally logging into my Match.com account."

Viola was draped over her couch, her face screwed up with stress. She had been working on her sequel. Really, she had. But it never quite seemed to come together. It wasn't that she lacked on inspiration now. She'd been thinking back to the Hardison barbecue all weekend. But every time that she started to think too deeply about it, her mind wandered away from the happy married couple and off to a steamy kitchen...

"I'll get the manuscript to you soon, Fran. Promise."

"Just remember the deadline," Francine reminded her. "If you keep me so tense like this, you'll turn my red hair gray."

She heard her agent flipping open another pack of cigarettes. The sound of a window cracking followed behind. *Smoking in her office again. Maybe she really was stressing Fran out.*

"You're already gray," Viola teased her. "I have it on good authority that you've been dying for years."

"Don't bite the hand that feeds you, love." But Vi could hear the smile in her voice.

"I'll get it to you soon; I really will," she promised. "I'm working on some new sources of inspiration. You're gonna get that manuscript in your inbox and you won't know what hit ya!"

"Alright, darling. We'll chat later."

The phone clicked off and Viola let her head drop back onto her couch pillow. She stared up at the ceiling, trying to lose focus in the maze of white popcorn spackle. Her fingers were shaking, and she buried them under her butt.

It was usually so nice to chat with Francine, even if she did have a deadline coming up. This time, though, she was starting to understand her agent's chain-smoking habit. The stress was unrelenting, and it only seemed to get worse the more that she thought back to that barbecue. Back to that cool glass of water and the boy with the soft half-smile...

She pulled the pillow over her face and let loose a little scream. Things had to ease up. And soon.

———

In Ruby's tiny living room, she, Viola, and a slew of bridesmaids sat cramped on the floor among an ever-growing number of wedding invitations. *The Bachelorette* played on the TV in the background while the girls drank wine, gossiped about friends, and took turns folding, licking, and stamping.

Viola had managed to steal a glass of pinot with her sister busy fielding wedding questions, and she'd even snagged the last chocolate chip cookie from a platter one of the girls had brought. Not the worst start to the night.

"He asked you to call him an Uber and pay for it? Drop that loser." Viola shook her head in disbelief as Ruby's cousin, Nadine, finished regaling the group with her latest story of a blind date gone bad.

Ruby playfully put a finger to her sister's lips. "Don't listen to the resident man-hater," she instructed. "Jordan brought you flowers, *and* he called before three days passed. I'd say he's worth a second chance."

"I am not a man-hater!" Viola smacked Ruby with an envelope in faux-horror. "I like plenty of men."

"Your cat doesn't count," Jessica, an old schoolmate, chimed in.

"Neither does your dad!" Someone called. The girls all collapsed into giggles.

"Ugh, if you can even count him." Viola rolled her eyes. Sometimes she wondered if she really liked her father at all, or if her relationship with him lasted only because of blood ties. Her mother was the parent who had bailed, but that didn't mean that her father was exactly the present one. His ever-revolving rotation of women, his vanity, his disinterest in the major events of Viola's life—it all left her feeling pretty empty.

Vi tabled the emotion and forced herself to laugh along with the rest of the group. It was already a kind of crummy day. No need to make it worse. She took a drink.

"I suppose that calling you a man-hater may have been a little bit of an over-characterization," Ruby admitted with a sly smile. "There is one guy who seems to have held the elusive Viola Reed's attention lately."

"Hey now, Brooks and I are definitely just friends," Viola assured them. She could feel her cheeks turning pink. "We stayed up the other night having a full-blown argument about whether *Star Wars* or *Star Trek* was the better franchise. I called him a butthole at least once. That's ultimate friend-zone."

"Sounds like a term of endearment to me," Nadine joked, putting a hand over her heart and fanning herself.

"Was *Star Wars* or *Star Trek* the victor?" Ruby asked.

"If you really have to ask me, then I might call you a butthole, too."

Viola laughed along with the rest of the group. She took a long draw of her wine. Once again, she knew that she was probably drinking just a little too much, and she could feel the effects. The world was turning soft and fuzzy and much happier than usual. A warmth grew in Viola's chest, spreading out to her fingertips and toes. Maybe butthole was a term of endearment, but who really cared?

The low hum of *The Bachelorette* on the TV was pressing up against her brain, giving her a dull headache. Ruby leaned over to her privately, a look of concern on her face. Her eyes darted to the glass of pinot; Viola knew before she spoke that her sister was regretting not snatching the wine from her earlier.

"You ok?" Ruby asked.

Viola nodded. It didn't take Ruby voicing the concern for her to know what her sister was thinking. More and more lately, they'd been having the conversation about how Vi was overdoing it, how she needed to start to get things together. Usually, this came in the form of Ruby gently presenting her with local suitors. Subtext: it's time to grow up.

Across the room, Viola's phone started ringing in her purse. Viola scrambled up from the floor, nearly knocking over a large open bottle of wine into a pile of freshly stamped invitations. Ruby caught them just in time, the fine line between her eyebrows crinkling up with worry.

Viola dug through the mess of lipsticks and receipts to produce her cell phone. She flipped it open.

"Love notes from Brooks?" Jessica teased.

"No, it's Matt again." Viola could feel her face screw up as she read his message.

"Again?" Ruby asked, gracefully getting up from her own spot on the floor. "He texted before?" She snatched the phone from her sister before Viola could protest.

Ruby's eyes grew wide as she read the message. "*Dang*," she breathed. "Maybe I've had too much wine but this feels like something really serious." She cleared her throat and read aloud: "V: Thinking of you again. I wish I didn't miss you so bad."

Viola stole her phone back, turning off the screen and shoving it down into her purse. "Sounds like he's been drinking tonight, too."

"You're gonna text him back, right?" Jessica asked, looking a bit starry-eyed. "I can't remember the last time Garret said something half so romantic to me."

"Seriously!" Nadine agreed. "If you don't get on that I will."

Viola collapsed onto Ruby's couch, rubbing her face with the palms of her hands. They weren't wrong; Matt was definitely one of the good ones. He'd treated her well when they were together, and between the distance he'd given her and the sweet messages he'd sent, he was still proving his worth after they'd broken up.

The memory of Wayne and Kathy Hardison, arms clasped tight around one another as they danced to their wedding song, flashed through her mind like white-hot lightning. For the first time in a long time—maybe ever—

Viola was starting to think that maybe true love was real. Maybe it was out there, just beyond her reach. Maybe she could have it for herself.

She reread the message. V: Thinking of you again. I wish I didn't miss you so bad.

Her stomach twisted as she thought about throwing Matt's toothbrush away without a second thought. She'd cleared him out of her life as though he had never been there at all. The truth was, she hadn't considered him, hadn't *really* thought about him or missed him until he'd shown up at the brunch that day. But maybe there was room for her to change. If true love was out there, didn't she deserve some of it?

"Alright." She threw up her arms and turned to produce the phone once more. "I'll text him back."

The girls cheered as she typed in a response.

"Was Matt the boyfriend who looked like that one Avenger?" Someone asked.

"Mhmm," Ruby answered. "And to think, Viola was the one who broke up with him!"

Viola's text was sent, and she raised her phone in victory. "Somebody better toast me; I'm full-on adulting over here!"

They all raised their glasses in celebration. The conversation returned to idle gossip once more, with everyone returning to the fold, lick, stamp routine.

Meanwhile, Viola remained on the couch, re-reading her text to Matt over and over again. I miss you, too. Come over tonight around ten? Was the response too forward? Suddenly, she doubted herself. Viola took yet another swig of her wine, trying to drown her anxieties.

As usual, the alcohol worked splendidly. Soon, she was floating through the invitation-folding party, laughing at all the jokes and even commenting optimistically on the plot of

The Bachelorette. She was warm all over, dizzy with the giddiness of the evening.

"Hey," Ruby piped up. "I can't believe I almost forgot to show you ladies! I finished the muslin for my wedding dress. Now I can get started on the actual fun part of making my own gown. Wanna see?"

Naturally, the women all raised their glasses once more and cheered with excitement. Ruby turned to Viola. "My hands are full. Do you think you could go grab it from my bedroom?"

"Course!" Viola agreed with a happy, vapid smile.

As she thought of the impending wedding once more, her stomach took that now familiar tumble. She chugged down the remainder of her wine and paused for another fill up before standing up, glass still in hand. She swayed on her feet, feeling the sudden rush of a new headache. She put two fingers to her temple as she picked her way through the group of girls and over to the hallway.

The darkness of her path made Viola feel even more unsteady. She felt her way along the wall until she found Ruby and Scott's room. She flipped on the light, blinking in the brightness.

The mockup was carefully displayed on a mannequin in the corner of the room. Even in drab beige muslin, it was clear that the gown was going to be beautiful. Ruby had always had an eye for fashion and sewing, and she'd truly outdone herself this time. A long, billowy cape pooled on the floor. Light, airy sleeves were perfectly placed to expose a thin strip of skin. The neckline dropped into a deep V, sure to make Ruby look even taller and more statuesque than she already was. The dress was absolute perfection.

Viola stumbled forward, reaching out to touch the fabric.

"*Shoot.*" Her wine glass had drooped forward, the deep burgundy liquid spilling like blood all over the cape. Viola snatched up the material, holding the muslin up to eyeball it in the light.

The buzz of the wine was wearing off the longer she looked at her awful mistake. She held the dress carefully, almost reverently, as she walked back down the hall. She could feel the red hot burn of her cheeks and hung her head in shame.

"It took me forever," Ruby was explaining. "But I wanted to get the details just right. I spent—"

She cut off as she turned, taking in the sight of her sister holding the sad pile of sopping red fabric. The color drained from her face.

"I'm so, so sorry," Viola started. She could hear that her words were slow and slurred, but she could do nothing. "It was an accident."

Ruby made no move to comment. She simply walked up to Viola, taking the dress in her arms and heading for the bathroom sink.

Viola followed her, tripping over her own feet. "You have to forgive me, Roo," she started once more, watching her sister scrub in the hot water. "I was just drinking so much because of Matt's message and I—"

Ruby turned, her face hard and still. "I thought I knew what to expect when I asked you to be my Maid of Honor," she said. "You've always been disorganized. A little chaotic. But I thought I could make up for that."

"No," Viola insisted. "I can fix this. Really—"

Ruby closed her eyes and put up one finger. "Just stop."

Viola had never seen her sweet, soft-spoken sister look this way before. Her stomach churned as she reflected on the magnitude of her situation. Ruby ran her hands through her long, blonde hair as she thought. Finally, she spoke.

"You have to get it together," she decided. "Go to an AA meeting or something. I can even find one for you."

Viola balked. "An AA meeting? Come on—"

"You have to step it up or you can't be my Maid of Honor," Ruby announced, her eyes flaring. Viola's stomach took an icy dip. "No more childish antics. No overindulging. It's time to grow up."

Viola nodded. She could feel tears burning in the corners of her eyes. "Do you think Scott could give me a ride home?"

Turning away from her, focusing completely on her dress, Ruby absently nodded. "I think that's a good idea."

Viola stepped out of the bathroom. She headed back to the living room, where the rest of the girls silently went about their business of folding, licking, and stamping. She collected her purse and headed toward the front door. She let herself out, knowing Scott would be shortly behind after Ruby sent him for her.

She opened her purse, pulling out her phone once more. Under a heart emoji sent by Matt, she composed another message. Let's make that nine instead.

Chapter 12

Viola could hardly hear herself think as she walked up the steps to her apartment building. Usually, she loved living in this part of Atlanta for its quieter residents and easy-going nearby offices. Now, though, she was suddenly aware of every annoying little noise. The ticking of the crosswalk light. The loud rap music coming from a car down the street. Worst of all, the hammering beat in her own chest, a sound that echoed around in her drunken head until she wanted to puke.

She practically raced up the stairs, more than ready to see Matt. She needed to stop this feeling. She needed to throw herself into something new.

And then there he was. Matt—bright-eyed, beautiful Matt with his innocuous smile—was at her front door waiting, one rose, long-stemmed and delicate, in his right hand. "You would not believe how many florists in my trashy downtown neighborhood don't keep 24-7 hours. They've gotta rethink that business model."

Viola was kissing him before he could laugh at his own joke. He was caught off guard, his eyes going wide. She turned, fumbling for her keys to unlock the door and let them inside. She took the flower and tossed it on her side table. Her thoughts were so loud and obnoxious, cutting through her alcohol-induced haze. She wanted to drown out everything stupid she'd done, drown out the deadline from Francine, drown out all the strange, stupid complicated feelings she'd been having.

The apartment was dark and quiet. It fed Viola's unease, and she turned to Matt with eyes that pled for a distraction. His shadowy face looked eager, ready to deliver.

With the door firmly closed behind them, Matt pushed Viola up against the wall. He kissed his way up her neck, leaving a tingling trail where his lips had touched. He smelled so familiar, so good. As she had a million times before, she thought of old leather and freshly mown grass as she kissed him back hazily.

The wine was really going to her head now. She felt a surge of confidence, propelling her forward and pushing her toward him. She wanted to bury the night at Ruby's house. She wanted to forget about responsibility for one, blissful moment. She kissed him harder, slipping her hands into his and intertwining their fingers.

Matt surprised her then, lifting her up to toss her on the couch. A surprised Duncan was scared from his shadowy spot on a pillow, and he yelped as he hopped down onto the ground.

"C'mon, Dunc, really?" Matt flipped on a lamp and knelt to pick up the cat. All memory of pain was forgotten as Duncan turned his attentions to the familiar visitor, his eyes shiny and round as he started to beg for a snack. Matt held out the cat for Viola to take, trying to his best to mask his impatience.

"Not tonight, bud," Viola said, scooping him up. Duncan

twisted in protest as she carried him down the hall, setting him on her bed to wait out her night. "Where were we?" she called, returning to Matt.

Standing in the light of the lamp, Matt looked happy and excited. His grin was lopsided, and his hair was mussed. He slipped off his coat, placing it on her countertop.

Shoot, Viola thought. He was wearing the t-shirt. It was the one he'd gotten as a gift from his brother a few months back that bore the classy phrase "Beer Hunter." She had thought that it might have been thrown away on his move out. She had never liked it. Matt and his brother called these novelty shirts their "bro shirts." They'd exchanged similar gifts on every major holiday. Viola had hated them all.

She had thought about those shirts the day after he left. She'd opened up her closet, seen her familiar mess of cardigans and sweaters, and felt a sense of relief that Beer Hunter was on its way out, never to return.

Now, she reached forward to touch her lamp, setting it on a dimmer setting. She ignored the shirt. Matt still looked great, she thought. The tousled hair really did things for her, as did the thick stubble that he'd grown after their breakup. Viola reached forward, stroking his jawline with her thumb.

Matt's eyes sparkled in response. He pulled her toward him then, kissing her once more. She felt her knees go weak, and she clutched his arms to stay upright. He helped her out of her coat, tossing it behind him before proceeding to kiss her neck again. She was surprised at just how much she had missed this.

Viola fumbled for the couch behind her. Her fingers found something soft and thick. She turned, briefly, and realized it was a jacket that Brooks had left behind from the night before spent watching movies together. She stashed it under a pillow. She didn't want to think about Brooks right now.

Matt surprised her then, picking her up once more to lay down on the couch. He leaned over her, stopping his kiss to reach a tentative hand out to touch her cheek.

"You have no idea how badly I've wanted this," he said, his voice low and quiet. "You were the one who got away. My friends kept telling me I had to shut up about you or go do something about it. I'm so glad we got back in touch."

"Me, too." Viola smiled up at him.

Her mind, though, had gone somewhere else. Matt's familiar smell of leather and cut grass had been overpowered by something sweeter, something even more intoxicating. And as Vi closed her eyes, it was no longer Matt kissing her but...

Brooks?

Her hand darted under her pillow and immediately found the jacket that Brooks had left behind from their last evening spent together. She could smell the sweet and spicy notes of his cologne still clinging to the fabric, a permanent part of him that he had left behind. The scent made her feel dizzy all over again. *Cut it out!*

"I can be your friend," Matt was saying. "Or I can be more. But I really, really hope you want more, like I do..."

He leaned forward then, kissing her once more. And with his touch, Viola found herself transported away...

A flash in her mind's eye: Brooks, swing-dancing with her at Hannah's wedding. Brooks, sending electricity sparking out from his fingertips as he guided her by the small of her back around the dance floor. Brooks, charming her and laughing with her and bucking all of the literary stereotypes she had boxed him into on night one of their meeting.

Was it possible? Could she really be—

Viola sat up suddenly, a hand on Matt's chest. He looked taken aback, his cheeks flushing pale pink.

She wanted easy, she reminded herself. Matt was a familiar pattern that she could step back into without a second thought. The fireworks, the passion, it was all extraneous. She just needed a warm body, and maybe if she committed to him again, she could have companionship without all of the romantic expectations that came from casual dating. She definitely, 100%, absolutely *did not* need Brooks Hardison.

But her stomach flipped upside down again, betraying her. She felt her own cheeks blush and was sure she must have turned bright red.

"I just remembered," she started, avoiding Matt's eyes. "I have some work I need to get done. I completely forgot about this assignment from Francine, and she's going to kill me if I'm late."

The happy, wild light behind his eyes faded down a level almost immediately. But ever the southern gentleman, Matt nodded and combed down his wild, tangled hair, working to regain his composure. "Of course," he agreed, trying to cover his disappointment with a brief smile. He got up from the couch and picked up his coat, placing it over his arm. He started for the door when he thought better of it, turning back to Viola once more. He crinkled up his nose, half-smiling. "Vi, are you absolutely sure you don't—"

"I'm sorry, Matt," she intoned. "Just not tonight."

He nodded, taking another step toward the door. "Alright. But let's do this again. I really think we can be great."

She nodded, trying to smile. Her stomach was churning. "Sure."

She followed Matt out, waving at him as he started down the apartment stairs. She shut the door loudly, throwing her back up against the frame as she tried to get her bearings. She shook her head in an effort to clear it, wishing again that she hadn't guzzled down so much wine.

Feeling more than a little stupid, Viola returned to the couch to retrieve Brooks' jacket. She held it between her fingertips, remembering all the time they had been spending together lately.

She threw it back down, went to the fridge, poured herself a glass of wine, and started pacing. *Nope. Nuh-uh.* She shook her head, even though there was no one there to watch her. *Not gonna fall for it, buddy.* I'm smarter than this.

But then she found herself picking the jacket back up again, smelling the lingering scent of him as it infiltrated every corner of her home.

And something clicked.

All at once, she realized what an idiot she'd been. She'd been writing stories about lovers who pined for each other through war time, kissed in the middle of a storm, or ran away together across the country. In all that time, in all her years of feeling cynical and hardened, it had never once occurred to her that love could be something quieter. It could be a joking conversation at a reception table. Quick car drives with the windows down. Arguing over sci-fi franchises.

Seriously, how is it she still had such a monumental following for her crappy romance novels?

Viola knew what she wanted to do then. It was out of character. It was nothing she'd ever done before. But she felt the compulsion from deep within her, driving her to ignore an entire adulthood of habit and go out on a limb. She grabbed her purse from the spot where she dropped it by the door. She found her phone quickly and started to compose a new message to Brooks.

She couldn't help but notice that her fingers were a touch shaky. Should she stop writing the message? Remember that girl who was so committed to ignoring these feelings just a few minutes before?

My place tomorrow?

She set the phone down carefully on the counter, willing herself not to obsessively check the screen as she waited for a reply. She walked the hallway back to her room, letting Duncan out. He flew by her in an orange blur, making a beeline for the kitchen to beg for more snacks. She laughed and followed him, trying to remember if she had any leftover sesame chicken from two nights before.

When the phone went off, she raced back to grab it up.

Did you forget the Martinez wedding?

... Of course Viola had forgotten the Martinez wedding, just as she forgot all dates and times in her life. Her fingers flew across the keyboard.

Drive together?

Her chest felt odd, and she put a hand to her heart. It beat fast and frantically, pounding on her fingertips as though trying to make its way out of her body.

Feeling stupid again, she realized: this was her heart racing. Ok, so maybe one or two of the love stories she wrote about were true. Viola laughed out loud. Her phone buzzed again.

I wish. I'm set to be an usher. I'll set aside some of the good snacks for you. ;-)

See you then, she wrote back.

She wasn't entirely sure what she was feeling because this was all new, but Viola could feel a silly, sappy smile on her face. She didn't care because she wanted to see what this went. Duncan sidled up to her on the counter, rubbing his body up and down her arm to ask for more snacks. She leaned forward, kissing his face. He meowed in surprise, looking disgruntled, but she satiated him with a generous helping from the refrigerator cat food.

She yawned, feeling suddenly very tired. It was getting late, and she knew that she needed to sleep. Especially, she thought, now that she had some important plans for the next day.

She turned off her lamp once more, letting the room slip back into darkness. All was quiet. The blinds were still up, as Viola always had them when she wrote during the day, and she left them that way, enjoying the feeling that the city might spy on her looking happy and excited for once rather than focused and skeptical. In the blue of the night, the skyline lights came in sparkling, casting tiny glowing fireflies onto her wallpaper. She didn't know that she was really going to get much sleep, but she didn't care.

Chapter 13

For the first time in her life, Viola wished that she owned more dresses.

She had scoured her closet for at least an hour, trying on more outfits than an 80s movie montage. The dresses she'd worn to past weddings made her feel inauthentic and uncomfortable, and the rest of her wardrobe was made up largely of different-colored yoga pants and hoodies. The task ahead of her felt impossible.

Finally, Viola had settled on a short black dress she'd only worn once or twice. It was simple. More her style. She put it on and stood in front of her mirror, allowing her sleek black hair to fall in heavy waves around her bare shoulders.

She turned, admiring the deep brown of her arms. The subtle slant to her chocolate eyes. The fullness of her hips.

For the first time in a long time, she felt truly beautiful.

Every day before work, she would roll out of bed, toss her hair up into a messy bun, and pull on her cleanest pair of stretchy pants before wandering out of her room to go write by the window. It felt unreal to think that this version of herself had been buried this whole time. She'd written about a million leading ladies with perfect porcelain skin, long eyelashes framing honeydew eyes, and bodies that curved in all the right places. But none of them had felt as real as the girl looking back at her in the mirror right now.

Dress on and ready to go, she slipped Duncan a treat before heading out the door.

She tagged along to the Martinez wedding with Scott and Ruby, who had put the muslin crisis behind her and was back to her usual bubbly self. Viola's sister peppered her with questions about Matt and their late-night tryst, eager to discover if her sister would soon be heading to weddings with her own plus-one.

Viola barely heard Ruby. She nodded along at all the right conversation beats, but she was transfixed on the blurry scenery passing by the car window as she wondered how the night's meeting would go. What would she possibly say? How could she get the courage to take charge? Her heart skipped ahead a little faster, pounding out a steady rhythm in her chest.

After a small eternity, the trio finally arrived at the Martinez wedding. Scott ran around the car to help the ladies out, and they walked together up to the stately front doors of a tall and intimidating cathedral.

They entered the chapel to the soft sounds of Edith Piaf's "La Vie En Rose" being played by a string quartet. Viola stood on her tiptoes as she walked, scouring a sea of traditional Southern wedding fascinators to spot a familiar usher's dark head. She had no luck, though, and took her seat in a central pew alongside her sister.

"Is everything alright?" Ruby whispered, leaning in to put a gentle hand on Viola's thigh.

Viola knew that she was sweating and figured she must look more than a bit harried. Ruby's mind was probably flashing back to the wine-stained muslin. "Completely." Viola smiled and squeezed her sister's hand back.

The guests had all taken their seats as the string quartet shifted into a slow and dreamy arrangement of Bob Dylan's "Make You Feel My Love." A tiny flower girl wearing a taffeta dress and flower crown skipped merrily down the aisle throwing soft, pale pink rose petals. The bridesmaids and groomsmen followed, each looking carefully manicured without a hair out of place. Finally, the bride, a vision in creamy white, floated her way to the altar, her joy radiating out to the guests.

This was the moment. The music, the flower petals, the chapel. It wasn't her wedding, but Viola couldn't have written the scene any better herself. She turned away from the beginning of the ceremony, scanning the crowd for Brooks and knowing for a certainty that she would find him. He'd probably be stashed in a back pew, his tie perfectly in place and his crushed black velvet suit pristine. His funny little half-smile peeping out as he took in the beauty of the wedding ceremony.

But Viola never saw him. She stole as many glances as she could, but she could never find him sitting in the crowd. Finally, she turned back to the vows. Her heart had picked up at an even faster pace.

When the ceremony was over, Viola excused herself from Scott and Ruby and hurried her way over to the reception hall alone. Here, too, the world was a dream. Long, spindly candles were placed with care on silk-draped tables. Greenery occupied every spare space and corner, with delicate ferns placed by the entrance to welcome guests inside. From the ceiling hung a million twinkling lights, transporting Viola to the peace of the outside.

And it was in the midst of all that, Viola finally spotted

him. He had somehow made it into the reception hall before her and even found his way to the bar. He sat alone at a table, a half-drunk water placed before him.

Viola's heart was impossibly fast, threatening to leap through her mouth and onto one of the ferns. She put a hand to her chest, smiling and trying to slow her breathing. She took her first steps in Brooks' direction, nervous but excited about what lay ahead of her.

She was interrupted by someone who had bumped into her. Viola turned to find a towering brunette who was about to drop two carefully balanced cocktails.

"Oh, no!" The girl jerked forward, desperately clinging to the glasses as the dark liquid splashed past the rim.

"I've got you!" Viola snatched up one of the drinks, saving it just in time before it came crashing down on the fine blue silk of the girl's dress.

... Unfortunately, the drops had ended up on Viola's dress instead. She had a small red-soaked patch in the center of her abdomen. She forced herself to forget it, though. She wasn't going to let one small accident throw off her night. This was her moment.

"Oh, no, your dress! One of those drinks had red wine. Those stains are a beast," the girl fretted over her spill, licking her thumb and attacking the fabric like there was any shot of saving the damaged silk.

She was almost painfully beautiful, with large, round eyes and a wide mouth full of pearly white teeth. Her thick, smooth hair had been wrapped into an expert knot at the top of her head, emphasizing high, pronounced cheekbones. "I think I'm just making it worse. And to think, that could've been me. I think you're basically my hero. I'm Emily. Please, you've got to let me buy you a drink or something. Come sit with me."

"Viola Reed," she introduced herself. "And I'm all good, really. I've got to go meet my friend at the table he got for us."

She started to walk off, but Emily stepped in tandem with her. "Come on, not even a quick cocktail? I think this Prada cost more than my first car. You really saved me."

"You're so sweet." Viola smiled and waved her off. "But really I'm fine."

She had reached Brooks' table, and he turned, finally seeing Viola for the first time all evening. Her breath caught in her throat.

How had she ever considered him average?

In a room full of crowded people, he was a presence to be noticed. His broad, strong shoulders moved powerfully under the thin cream of his button-down. The lights glinted off the softness of his curls, creating a halo effect around his head. His smile was so relaxed and authentic. It overtook his whole face, creating happy little lines around his eyes and pink swells on his cheeks.

Viola smiled back.

"Oh hey, you two already met each other!"

Viola's smile faltered as Brooks reached around her to take one of the glasses from Emily. The girl swept past her, her long dress brushing on Vi's legs as she took her seat next to Brooks.

"I'm glad you volunteered to get the drinks. This waiter is proving impossible to flag down." Brooks took a drink from his glass and then offered the rest to Viola. "Here, Reed. Take the rest of mine until we can get you one, too."

Viola felt a nervous pit forming in her stomach as she stepped around the side of the table to find a seat of her own. "I'm sorry," she started. The words felt heavy and awkward in her mouth. "I think I missed something."

Brooks grabbed Viola's hand, his face stretching out into that big grin again. "This is Emily Norman. *That* Emily that everyone kept telling me about, remember? I finally met her during wedding prep and we just kind of hit it off. We blew off the wedding to come hang out and talk."

Emily blushed, the delicate pink stain bringing out the green in her eyes. "Brooks is too kind. He let me tag along with him when I didn't know anyone else at the wedding. And then he spared me from having to make ceremony small talk."

"That's great." Viola's voice sounded small and echoey in her ears. She wasn't sure if she was smiling back.

"Let me go get you your own drink," Emily started, standing back up. "You two should catch up."

"Oh, I'm fine—" Viola started.

"I insist," Emily said, reaching out to squeeze Viola's shoulder. "It's the least I can do."

And with that she was off. The crowd seemed to part at her command as she slipped through, leaving the subtle sweet scent of fig and caramel in her wake. It made Viola feel sick.

"Well?" Brooks asked, leaning back in his seat. The big, stupid grin just wouldn't go away.

"Well." Viola repeated, forcing her own small smile.

"She's great, right? Definitely a step up from the usual bimbos I've picked up in the past. And she's never seen any *Star Trek*, can you believe that? Killer first date in the making."

Viola cleared her throat. She tried for a joke. "Only buttholes like—"

"Yeah, only buttholes like *Star Trek*." Brooks laughed and took Viola's hand again. "Do me a favor and hang out with us for a bit? I don't want to mess this one up and you're my resident romance expert."

"Definitely not an expert," she mumbled.

"Reed, come on." He smiled at her. "You changed my whole outlook. All your cynical talk of clichés and stereotypes might get old, but it's all true. I'm going to get serious, pursue something more than a different bridesmaid every wedding."

"So you decided to start with a bridesmaid at *this* wedding."

"What can I say? Old habits die hard." He grinned, the fine lines around his dark eyes deepening. "She's really something though."

"For sure." Viola tried to smile back. Her mouth felt dry and tasted sour. She reached with shaking fingers for one of the water glasses scattered around the table.

"I didn't want to seem like an idiot when I told you about Chelsea," Brooks was fiddling with his napkin and shaking his head. "I don't know, maybe you were right when you called me out for not wanting to own up to a broken heart. But the truth is, it took me a really long time to get over what happened with her. But I think I'm finally there. And it's all thanks to you, Vi."

He reached across the table and took her hand. Viola forced herself to smile. What a wonderful wingman she had turned out to be.

Emily returned to the table, a fresh cocktail in hand. She slid it across the table and then took her seat again. Viola couldn't help but notice how close they were sitting, with Brooks' shoulder just brushing hers.

"I hope it's not too fruity for you," Emily said. "This wedding did themed cocktails. I think this was called an 'Apple-y Ever After Martini.' Isn't that the cutest?"

"The cutest," Viola agreed. She cut a look over at Brooks, who was too starry-eyed to notice. Viola took the drink and pulled it toward her as a bright, brassy tune kicked on over the loud speakers.

Brooks smacked the table with both hands, clearly excited. "Time to show off!" He declared. He offered a hand to Emily, who took it, and they both stood up. "You can thank Reed here for showing me some swing dance moves."

"Ooh, fancy." Emily laughed. "I'm afraid I might be a disappointment on the dance floor, though. Two left feet."

"Not a chance," Brooks said. "I'll show you the ropes."

The pair glided off toward the dance floor, his arm curving around to rest on the small of her back. Viola took a swig of her drink as she watched them. It went down too bitter and made her sputter and choke.

Two left feet. Sure. Viola knew how these things went. She'd written about a million Emilys in her novels. Beautiful, sweet, genuine. She'd move like an angel, and the whole room would be watching. Viola had shown Brooks the dance, but Emily would reinvent the practice.

Vi had come to the wedding relishing in all the little details. The romantic music had been a soundtrack to her heart. The decorations swept her away to her own fairy tale. She'd even felt like she looked the part, with the pretty dress and the hair and the makeup. But she knew now that she had misread the details. This wasn't her love story.

It was someone like Emily's.

Chapter 14

"I'm so glad we're doing this." Matt was smiling at her from where he sat across from her in their bowling lane.

Viola had to admit it: she was glad, too. It had come as a relief to have a little company after *to*night. It had come as no surprise when Brooks had asked to bail on their plans to spend some more time with Emily after the Martinez wedding. Vi had been desperate for company, and so she'd called Matt.

She felt silly and a bit stupid. What had she been thinking? The dress, the racing heart, the nerves. Honestly, it was like she had become one of the insipid characters she wrote about in her novels. No wonder Francine had told her that her work had become so predictable and boring. She had clearly become engrossed in it and let the fantasy world infect her reality and twist things.

And to make matters worse, she'd gone to a *wedding* for inspiration to change things up? Viola was losing her grip on things.

She was grateful for Emily, really. She'd lifted a veil off of her eyes, helped her to see things as they really were. With someone like Emily in the picture, the world was back in order for Viola again. There was peace in that. Comfort.

And ultimately, the Emily situation had led her back to Matt. Sweet, funny, handsome Matt. Maybe he could be Viola's inspiration. There had to be some dignity in returning to someone who was so good for her. And that never happened in any of her books. The leads always stayed together through thick and thin; they never "took a break" or straight up broke things off at the prospect of long-term commitment. This could be her original new story. There was a commentary about maturity somewhere in there.

Right?

Anyway, it felt good to be around him. Matt clearly wanted to be with her. He'd come over right away to pick her up from the reception and they'd decided to go bowling, her still in her cocktail dress and everything. He'd eaten it right up, cracking jokes about how people would think he was underdressed. Matt made Viola laugh, and she found that she could table her feelings from the rest of the night, square them away in a quiet little place inside of her where she didn't have to confront them. All she had to do now was bowl.

"I'm glad we're doing this, too." She agreed with him, smiling back.

"Honestly, I was surprised you were taking a night off from Jean-Luc, the shirtless wonder." Matt smiled, raising an eyebrow at her. "It would seem that you've changed since we last talked, Vi."

Viola's stomach did a little flip at Matt's deliberate mention of her book, but she ignored it. She smiled back. "Don't get too excited. I'm only taking a little inspiration break."

"Just picture a life with me," he joked, hands in the air to paint a picture of what could be. "Barefoot, pregnant, eating bon-bons on the couch instead of going gray over deadlines and character arcs."

"Hey, that gray hair I found that one time was an isolated incident." She smirked, falling back into their familiar banter.

"So." He pronounced, sitting down at the computer chair to type in their names. "Should we go ahead and put you in as LOSER and me in as WINNER, or do you prefer something more subtle?"

"My first name will work fine, thanks." She laughed.

"Don't think that I forgot your track record with bowling, baby bumpers." Matt picked up a ball, suppressing a laugh of his own as he tested its weight. "You're the only person I've ever bowled with to score a perfect zero."

"You're doing nothing to help your case in getting back together with me," Viola teased.

"You're here, aren't you?" He smiled at her before he stepped up to bowl his first round. "I don't think I'm doing too shabby."

He swung the ball, which went flying down the lane in a perfect spin of blue and purple. *Strike.* Matt swung around, fists pumping in the air like a little kid. "Still got it!"

It was cute to watch Matt acting so giddy. He was undeniably handsome, traditionally so. Viola had always thought that Matt would work well as hero material, and she'd modeled characters in her novels after him on more than one occasion. He was charming, too, with the easy, open disposition and the willingness to look a little silly.

Still, she felt that pang in her chest. She willed the emotions of her night back further down inside of her. She smiled at Matt before standing up to go pick up her own ball and take her turn.

It was just a bit too heavy, and she felt rather silly shuffling it along to the approach area in her too-long dress. In her efforts, her greasy red bowling shoes caught on the fabric, and she tripped forward, just catching herself before she could take a tumble. Matt was beside her in an instant. He bent down and rolled the hem for her, producing a safety pin from his pocket to expertly pin it up and out of the way.

"You just casually carry safety pins around?" She asked, one eyebrow raised.

"Are you going to question my act of charity?" Matt smiled. He stood up, brushing his hands off on his pants. He put a hand to her elbow, helping to guide her forward. "Better, right?"

Viola nodded, pursing her lips. At the feeling of his touch, her mind had drifted to somewhere else, to someone else. She remembered the sparks sent racing up her skin at the scant trace of Brooks' fingers. The new dizziness to her gait that had left her unsure and unsteady. The burning she had felt in her chest as she would try not to look up at him.

But she had felt something with Matt just now, too. *Right?* There was a reason that she had wanted to kiss him that night in her apartment. That she wanted to lose herself in him and let him erase that someone else still lingering at the back of her mind. There was an undeniable compulsion that she felt to be with him now. She simply couldn't let herself forget it.

Viola shoved down the other feelings. She ignored them, vowing never to let them surface and find life again.

She had to be honest with herself. Viola had changed, whether she liked it or not. She could see her life now as an outsider might: how she threw the emotional turmoil of her childhood as well as her own adult insecurities into the written word. How she'd written out love story after love story not because her readers fed into bull crap as she liked to attest, but rather because she was righting the wrongs of her own story.

And it was because she'd done so much writing and not enough real living that she'd fallen for the wrong archetype. Brooks was a side character, just as she'd originally thought. He was a footnote. The best guy friend. Someone that Viola could help to fix and to grow as she, herself, grew up a little, too. Writing romance had certainly taught her that the leading lady doesn't end up with the basket case. She doesn't have an epic fairy tale with the boy who might shine, but only after a little work. She ends up with the prince. With someone like Matt.

He was good for her. *He* was the kind of guy who dropped what he was doing and picked her up after one quick phone call. *He* wanted her.

Matt's hand was still at her elbow, there to help if Viola needed it. *The spark would come,* she assured herself. If she could grow to recognize that love was real and very much worth having, then she could grow to recognize its manifestations as they really were. She didn't need butterflies or a racing heartbeat. She needed devotion, care, attention. *She would make this work.*

"I think I've got it now," she smiled at Matt and stepped forward to bowl her ball.

She raised it and took four steady paces toward the approach line, letting it fly out of her fingers and onto the lane with a satisfying *thud*. The pins crashed, flying everywhere.

"*Yes!*" Viola spun around, ecstatic. "I'm sorry; what were you saying earlier about baby bumpers?"

Matt stuck out his tongue and retrieved his own ball from the return. He hip-bumped her out of his way as he walked by, winking. "Settle down, Lebowski. The game is just starting."

He surprised her then, planting a quick kiss on her mouth. Viola was taken aback, and she withdrew, her fingertips brushing her lips.

"I took you off guard," Matt said, his eyes wide. "I'm so sorry. I think I just thought because of the other night and the way we've been flirting that you wanted to—"

She grabbed his shoulders and pulled him back, kissing him long and deep. She was going all in. She needed to go all in.

The sound of catcalls from the rowdy team beside them brought Viola back down to earth. She pulled away, wiping away the kiss with the back of her hand before sliding her hands into his back. Someone in the group wolf-whistled, and she gave them the finger without ever even looking their way. Nothing was going to ruin this. Matt rested his forehead on hers, the heavy bowling ball still cradled in his hands between them.

"Wow, Vi." His voice came out soft and husky. "You have no idea how long I've wanted to feel this way again."

She half-smiled at him and kissed him once more before pulling away. She crossed her arms, suddenly feeling too cold in the bowling alley AC. "You keep bowling," she instructed. "I'm going to go get us something to drink."

She left their station and made her way over to the bar.

The boy filling drinks looked barely old enough to serve, with a face full of acne and a mouth full of silver and red braces. Viola noticed that the shoe rental service was located at the same bar just down the counter from the beer tap, and the boy stood spraying scented aerosol into pair of elevens right beside the clean glasses. Yuck. It took a lot of effort to silence her inner health inspector.

Viola swallowed down the ick factor and stepped forward. "Two beers, please."

The young barkeep pulled two cloudy glasses out and filled them for her. He slid them across the counter and Viola retrieved them, leaning forward to take a deep pull from her glass.

She didn't know how it happened so quickly, but somehow she had finished the glass in just a few swallows. She chased it with the other beer in her hand and slid the glasses back across the counter to the boy. "Two more."

Viola could picture Ruby's face. She could envision her sitting on a greasy bar stool right next to her, silently counting the emptied glasses. Viola knew that she was over-doing it again. She was letting herself slip back into the shadowy place. She was backtracking.

But give her some credit, Ruby! She'd had a weird night. She deserved a drink. Or a few drinks. Besides, she had displayed enough maturity for a while by returning to Prince Matt, the wonderboy everyone had been urging her to date again for ages.

Viola wiped her mouth with the back of her arm and grabbed the two newly filled glasses. She shuffled over to Matt at their lane, enjoying the warm looseness that was just beginning to set in after her drinks at the reception and now at the alley.

"You didn't get another strike while I was gone, right?"

"I save my showing off strictly for when you're around to watch." He smiled, swinging up his ball to go again.

She took a seat, cupping her glass in both hands as she

watched Matt bowl. She felt a vibration in her pocket and knocked back another swallow before setting down the beer to pull out her phone. It was Brooks.

Sorry I bailed. 😬 *Grab some brunch together tomorrow?*

The knot in her stomach returned, writhing and twisting. She forced it into submission with another long pull on her drink, finishing off her third glass. The pleasant warmth and looseness was beginning to morph into something closer to sickness. Viola rubbed at her temples before replying.

Yeah, course. Can I bring Matt?

She could see three little dots light up on her screen and knew that Brooks was replying. They disappeared and reappeared, and she wondered briefly if he had been interrupted in his writing by Emily saying something witty and charming. She might have wondered if her mentioning Matt had surprised Brooks, but she wasn't sure that he had even noticed with his current preoccupation. Finally:

I'll bring Emily. Sounds like a double.

Matt had finished his round and returned to the seating area, picking up his own drink to take a swallow. "Hey, you doing ok?"

"Doing great," Viola replied with a smile. "How would you feel about grabbing some brunch tomorrow?"

Chapter 15

E mily Norman was the kind of person who could spend her night drinking and dancing and still look magically unaffected. She had shown up to brunch with Brooks with her hair in neat, smooth plaits down her back. Her clothes were preppy and chic, definitely ironed. Her makeup was pristine.

Meanwhile, Viola felt like she'd been run over by a car. She knew that the dark circles under her eyes must make her look like she had been punched. Her hair was in the loose, messy bun that she reserved for days spent alone and writing. She'd put some effort into her clothes in light of her brunch date, but the moderately expensive jeans and collared shirt she'd scrounged up from her closet were nevertheless in desperate need of another wash. After the group made their introductions and pleasantries in the restaurant lobby, Viola hung behind everyone and desperately tugged at her top to try to reduce some of the embarrassment.

"Who's your fairy godmother, and how much are you paying her?" She jokingly asked Emily as they sat down at their table. "You look about a million times better than I do after a night of wedding drinks."

Emily blushed and waved her off. "You are too much! You look beautiful."

"You do," Matt agreed, sitting down beside her and slipping an arm around her chair.

"No, really," Vi insisted. "You've got that, uh, that *je ne sais quoi*." She winked in Brooks' direction, remembering the familiar line that he tried on her when they first met. *That thing that gives you the butterflies...*

"Is that a cat treat in your hair?" Brooks asked, leaning forward to retrieve something from Viola's bun.

Her ears burned as she snatched back something small and crunchy. Curse that Duncan. She had fallen asleep on the couch cuddling him.

She tried to shake it off. "So, where did you two end up last night?"

Brooks and Emily smiled at each other. Emily's face blushed a pale pink. "We took a walk by the river," she said. "It was so beautiful."

"You should check out the lake near my place next," Matt offered. "It's got the most incredible wildlife."

"Yes," Viola jumped in. She reached out and took Emily's hand. *Physical touch is a great way to build a connection.* "You should definitely do that next. It's so dreamy and romantic out there. Bring some wine and do a picnic."

She stole a glance in Brooks' direction. He looked taken aback by her approach to Emily; had he expected her to be rude? Withdrawn? Her hand was still lingering on Emily's, and she pulled it back as quick as she had reached it out. Hold on—had she just been using Brooks' playbook against him? Was she... trying to make him uncomfortable? Vi felt her face turn red again and she busied herself in unfolding her fancy cloth napkin. Whatever she was doing, she probably ought to cut it out.

The waitress arrived, handing out waters and menus. The group quieted for a moment, scanning the offerings.

"*Hey, Asian avocado toast sounds amazing!*"

The exclamation came out in unison. Brooks and Viola smiled at each other from across the table. Did he look a little awkward? His eyes had cast down quickly after they spoke in tandem, and he'd returned to his menu. Was she imagining that his ears had turned red?

She turned back to Emily, throwing herself into the conversation. "So, Emily, I've got to learn more about you. What do you do for a living?"

"Oh gosh, nothing interesting." She laughed, the sound tinkling and merry. "I manage a dental office. It's your typical nine to five, but I can tell you all about cavities and fillings. Plus, free veneers!"

"She's being modest," Brooks explained. "Emily manages a chain of dental offices."

"Wow," Viola commented. "Great job, beautiful girl, and enough dental insurance to ensure that your nineteen kids and counting all have straight, white teeth. Sounds like you hit the jackpot there, Hardison."

Emily giggled. "Nineteen kids and counting?"

"Ah, Fabio here hasn't told you yet that his playboy routine is all a gimmick to reproduce and create a new line of baby Super Hardisons? Get too close, and you'll find yourself barefoot and pregnant within a year."

Emily wrinkled her nose. "That's funny," she said. "But no kids for me. I'm a career type. I have a four-oh-wunk."

Viola suppressed a smile as she turned to Brooks, whose face had turned bright red at his date's misstep. *Four-oh-wunk? Or 401k?* She mouthed as Emily took a sip of her water. Brooks motioned for her to cut it out, but she noticed that he was smiling a small bit, too.

"I mean, don't get me wrong," Emily explained. "Kids are so cute. I'm, like, obsessed with my nieces. But travel sounds nice. So does having enough spare cash to actually buy a house or do some investing. Kids just aren't my preference. And also, why are they always mysteriously sticky?"

Viola snorted into her drink. "I can't fault you that," she said.

"So what about you, Vi?" Emily asked, nestling her chin on her propped hands as she took Viola in. "What do you do?"

"I write," she said. "Romance. It's silly stuff. Hallmark-y."

"It's kind of her superpower," Brooks said, smiling. "You should do the thing."

"The thing?" Matt asked, his face curious.

"I don't think anyone needs that much cynicism over breakfast." Viola waved him off.

"Come on, Reed!" Brooks grinned.

"Now I have to see it!" Emily chimed in.

"Alright, alright."

Viola sat back, crossing her arms as she sized up Emily all over again. She already knew exactly where Emily fit into the romance mold. It was so obvious, it almost felt silly to have to say it out loud.

She looked at Brooks then, who had so eagerly cheered her on. His eyes were searching for an answer. She knew it then. He was expectant, maybe even nervous. She could feel it. Was he looking for validation here? Did he want her to confirm that Emily was his Cinderella after all? That he had done good and outgrown playboy status? Viola made her verdict.

"You're a classic heroine," she pronounced. "You're beautiful. Accomplished. For all that we should want to hate you, but you're too nice for that."

The group laughed.

"Let me guess: you were an ugly duckling in high school and then you had a glow up? Pretty people aren't as nice as you without having a meaty backstory."

Emily laughed again. "I had scoliosis," she said. "Wore a back brace all through middle school."

"You did not." Viola was surprised at her own superpower.

"Hand to God!"

"What else?" Matt piped up, curious.

"Alright, let's get really specific..." Viola thought for a moment. "You've got a relative who's awful to you. All the pretty girls in romance novels have them. Usually a step-parent or stepsibling. Apparently being innately evil is a prerequisite for marrying into an existing fictional family."

"Stepmom. She hates me. Her name is actually Karen, just like the meme."

Brooks started clapping, his face split into a wide grin. "The Amazing Viola Reed, everyone! Call Brooks Hardison if you're interested in booking her for future events."

"Thank you, thank you."

She stole another glance at Brooks, who had slipped his hand into Emily's. Viola had said the right thing. Of course she had. This is what he wanted to hear, that he had finally found The Girl, and that they were destined for Love. That all the stars had aligned, and they were meant to be together. She was giving him what he wanted. She was giving him what he deserved.

Brooks was a great guy. That's all Viola had really been thinking when she had raced off to the Martinez wedding. He was her best friend, even more than Ruby or Hannah, and the realization had taken her by surprise, thrown her off balance. She hadn't known how to feel because she had never really felt that way about a boy before. She was going to give him exactly the person he deserved now, because he was wonderful and sweet and a great freakin' person.

And besides, Viola had Matt. She slipped her hand into Matt's hand, just as Brooks had with Emily. Matt turned, surprised at her spontaneous touch. He smiled at her and leaned over to kiss her cheek.

"Look at you two," Emily gushed. "You're like Baby and Johnny over there. Or Kim and Kanye."

Viola snorted. She stole a glance at Brooks, but he looked unphased by his date's pop culture reference and simply enamored with her instead. Viola swallowed down the instinct to be callous and sent Emily her most gracious smile for the compliment.

Matt was close and getting closer, Vi's hand in his gave him the sign he needed to cozy up. He went to kiss her on the cheek again, but this time she turned and kissed his mouth. Her stomach did a little flip as she heard Emily whistle. Sparks, she kept repeating to herself. This is what sparks felt like.

"Well, forgive me," Matt announced as he pulled back. "I'm gonna take care of some business in the little boy's room before the waitress gets back."

"Great idea," Emily agreed, standing up. "Me, too."

They left, leaving Brooks and Viola at the table alone together. He took a drink of his water. She fiddled with her cloth napkin.

"So, when did you—"

"How was last—"

They laughed again, the sound nervous and awkward. *Get it together, Reed. Just jump right in.*

"I was just going to say that Emily seems wonderful." Viola volunteered. "Way to buck my expectations, Hardison. Looks like you found Cinderella after all."

"She's definitely something," he agreed. "First date I've had in a long time that could keep up with my pithy jokes. Unless you count yourself."

"Definitely not," Viola waved him off, hoping he wouldn't notice the way her cheeks were flushing. "In the romance novel that is your life, I'd be cast as the sister character. Ooh, or maybe the grand oracle who shows you the way your life needs to go."

"I was thinking you might be my Ghost of Girlfriends Future, who shows me how pathetic my life could be if I keep dating Lindsay Lohan types?" He smiled and winked.

"Ah, yes." Viola agreed. "Or the crazy hag character, who almost makes you swear off women before your princess arrives on the scene."

"I don't know," Brooks said, shrugging. "I don't think a crazy hag character ever shows up to brunch with Liam Hemsworth on her arm."

Viola snorted. "Yeah, I got pretty lucky there."

"So how did that happen, anyway?" Brooks asked, swirling his glass of water. He looked so casual. Or at least, he was trying to look casual. She shouldn't care which way it was. She knew that. But Viola couldn't help but wonder if Brooks was the tiniest bit jealous.

"I thought you were still on the fence about him?" He asked her.

"I guess I figured that if you were going to grow up and mature, going to be a big boy who can go on a date with a real woman or something, that maybe I could do some growing up, too." She shrugged. She tried to smile, but the gesture came out feeling forced and strange. "You can't be the only one with a really good character arc."

"Well, he seems great." Brooks said. He looked up then, taking Viola off guard with the piercing intensity of his gaze. "And he seems to really care about you."

"He does," she answered, holding the eye contact. "I'm going all in. Giving it a real shot."

"Congratulations."

The silence between them was palpable. It was the first time Viola had ever been at a loss for what to say to Brooks. Conversation had always come so easy between them. She wanted to say something, *anything*. But the words weren't coming.

Thankfully, Matt and Emily made their returns, sliding back into their chairs with impeccable timing. The waitress followed, pad and pen in hand, to take their orders.

"Are you ready?" She asked them. "Know what you want?"

"Definitely," Viola piped up. "Knew the minute I sat down."

CHAPTER 16

WINTER

"I might have overdone it just a little bit."

Hannah emerged from her dressing room wearing a silk cocktail dress. Her arms were bright red, freckles standing at attention as dark blossoms on her skin. The spaghetti straps bit into her shoulders, leaving angry white marks. She grimaced as she did a little turn in front of the mirror for Ruby and Viola.

"I don't know, Han, I think this might be cosmic payback for all the bragging you did about spending a month in Aruba for that delayed honeymoon you took." Viola grinned.

Even Ruby stifled a laugh with one demure hand. "You still look beautiful. And I'm sure that Aaron will be too busy getting lost in your eyes to care about a little sunburn."

"Oh no, I want him to notice my pain," Hannah pronounced, slipping back into her dressing room. Viola expertly caught the dress as her friend flung it over the top of the door. "He was the one who fell asleep next to me on the beach and forgot to tell me to flip over."

As if on cue, Aaron popped his head around the corner

of the dressing room. "Are you ladies done? I could just about eat the north end of a southbound skunk."

"Close," Ruby laughed as she assured him. "I think Hannah just tried on our winning dress."

"No way!" Hannah called from her changing room. "You can't do this to me, Roo; I'll look like a lobster in all that cream."

"Come on, the burn will definitely be faded by the wedding," Viola said. "It's not until May."

"... Is it really that bad?" Aaron stage-whispered, his face cracked open like a jack-o'-lantern. "She still won't let me see her naked."

"She only looks vaguely related to Elmo." Viola smiled.

"I can hear you!" Hannah reminded her.

Bridesmaid shopping finally complete, the girls collected their things and emerged from the dressing room to join the boys. They'd spent all morning at the bridal and tux shop trying on various apparel, and Viola was completely exhausted by the effort.

She spotted Matt hanging out near the cash register, a sharkskin suit in hand. He looked uncomfortable and turned to her as soon as she walked up.

"You're sure they are ok with me tagging along today? I'm just a plus one."

"Trust me," Viola started, placing a hand on his arm comfortingly. "They might like you more than they like me. They're happy to have you along."

They had been seeing a lot of Matt lately. He had slipped back into Viola's life as though he had never left. Her desk had been moved to accommodate his Bowflex. Her closet had been rearranged for his t-shirts. Even a new blue toothbrush had made its home on her bathroom countertop.

Things were moving fast. Viola preferred it that way,

though. There was a lot going on in her life that she would rather be distracted from, and this was a pleasant escape. Her phone had been going off nonstop lately. The wedding plans with Ruby were piling up, drowning her in a mountain of spreadsheets and catering phone numbers. The deadline for Francine was swift-approaching, and Viola had finally conceded to let Matt close the laptop and shut the bay window so that she could breathe just a little.

And on top of it all, Brooks continued to text and call her. Viola still enjoyed it. She still smiled when she opened his messages and laughed when he sent over a gif or funny joke. But at least half the time, the text would be about what he'd been doing with Emily, how they were Instagram official and how they'd moved in together. With each of those messages, Viola would feel a rush of embarrassment remembering the Martinez wedding. When she was feeling really low, she wished that she could go all the way back and take back the night she first met Brooks. That was when she started to feel so vulnerable and confused.

Her phone went off again as she stood by the register with Matt. Viola pulled it out of her pocket and breathed a sigh of relief when she saw that it was her father reminding her of a get-together for the next weekend.

"More champagne before you go?"

A store employee dressed in a chic black turtleneck offered them a tray of drinks. Although they would never confirm it, Viola knew that Ruby and Hannah had specifically told the store staff to withhold any free drinks during their fitting appointment. This employee obviously hadn't been around for that discussion.

"*Yes, please.*" Viola snatched up her glass and downed it quickly, pinching the bridge of her nose as she tried to clear her mind.

"I'm good, thank you." Matt said.

The employee started to walk away with the tray, but Viola followed and scooped off Matt's glass, anyway. "I'll take his," she said with a wink, setting her empty first glass back on the tray.

She could feel Ruby's eyes on her from across the store. The drinking was getting worse. Viola knew that. But she couldn't stop it. Or maybe she just didn't want to. She had been enjoying the perpetual haze, the floating, far-away feeling she experienced when she kissed Matt or held his hand. She could ignore the phone calls this way. She could shove it all down, pretend that she had the world under control.

Besides, Matt seemed to like her this way, and wasn't he the one that mattered? Ruby and Hannah had been pushing her for so long to have a boyfriend. And here was one who liked easy-going Viola, who preferred the version of her that wasn't cynical or biting or worried about a deadline. That seemed reason enough to keep doing what she wanted.

She polished off the glass of champagne.

"I vote Chinese food," Hannah declared as she sidled up next to Viola, her new garment bag draped over her arm.

"Ugh, I can't take it anymore." Aaron rolled his eyes playfully. "That's all you have wanted for a week."

"Hey, you married me for better or for worse." Hannah shrugged, smiling. "So, Chinese anyone?"

"Sounds great to me." Ruby chimed in, stepping up to them with Scott by her side.

"Me too," Matt agreed.

"You're outvoted." Hannah stuck her tongue out at her husband and slipped her arm through his as they headed toward the exit.

Viola felt Matt put his hand on the small of her back,

guiding her toward the door. "Just a sec," she said. "I'm just going to run to the bathroom before we go. I'll meet you outside."

He nodded and followed the group as she lingered behind. When the door shut, she pulled her phone from her pocket, staring at the blank screen. Finally, she clicked it on and pulled up her messages.

Getting Chinese without you. :P

Her fingers hovered over the message. Viola held her breath as she clicked send.

Why had she sent Matt away before she could text Brooks? The action was clandestine. Private. She didn't want anyone to see her, but most definitely not her boyfriend. Viola knew that this line of thought probably merited more consideration, but she shoved down the instinct. She looked around for the girl with the champagne, holding onto a brief hope that she could steal one more glass.

Her phone buzzed.

You loser! You owe me. Lunch tomorrow? Noon? The place we went after Aaron's wedding?

Viola started to type, then deleted. She started over, her fingers carefully finding the keys. She didn't feel the same carefree ease of texting Brooks that she used to have. There were too many words she couldn't say for her to feel completely comfortable with him.

Are we doing a double?

His reply came quickly.

Nah, let's hang. I've got news. Talk tomorrow.

Viola pocketed her phone, letting her breath expel in one long, low sigh. She set off for the exit to join her friends.

Chapter 17

She had come to their Chinese restaurant ready to ice Brooks out. He had come with chocolates in hand and a sketch he'd drawn on a napkin of Duncan's eager little face.

Viola had consciously chosen to sit back in her chair, as far away from him as she could. She had ordered something she knew he wouldn't like so that there'd be no risk of him asking to share. She had looked him anywhere but in the eye, nearly memorizing the curve of his mouth and the strong line of his jaw.

But resistance was obviously futile.

Soon, Viola was laughing so hard that water was coming out of her nose. She clasped her hands to her face, trying desperately to save herself a little dignity as she continued to snort.

"I'm telling you, he was *orange*." Brooks grinned at her as she struggled.

Viola waved him off. "Please, stop! I can't take it anymore."

"Hey, it's all true," Brooks went on. "I even went so far as to ask him if I could take a selfie, but he said that he 'doesn't like his image to be reduced down to paper.'"

"*Stop!*"

He always knew how to break through with her, how to get past her walls. Brooks had been regaling her with stories of meeting his sister's new boyfriend, a vain, pretty type who had come to a family dinner earnestly quoting philosophy, wearing a Versace neck scarf, and sporting an obvious fake tan. Viola could hardly stand it; she'd been laughing since before the pot stickers came out. Now she couldn't get down a bite of her beef and broccoli without choking.

"Oh, man," she sighed, finally regaining a little control. "You shouldn't be allowed to tell funny stories over a meal."

"I've missed this." Brooks smiled at her. "Which, uh, leads me to my big news."

He looked down at his food then, stabbing at his chicken and noodles. Viola felt her stomach give a little twist, and she looked down, too.

"Of course," she said. "I've been dying to hear."

"Well, you know I've been dating Emily."

"No, I had completely forgotten about your sweet, funny, supermodel girlfriend." Viola tried for a laugh. It came out sounding hollow and fake. She opted for a smile, which he received with a look of relief.

"Her practice is moving her out to Charlotte. Giving her a big promotion. She's going regional."

"Regional? Wow, impressive." Viola raised her eyebrows. Her stomach flipped again, and she put down her fork. "Sounds like she'll be able to get all the veneers that she wants."

Brooks smirked. "Yeah, yeah."

"Charlotte. So that means…"

"It means that we break up," Brooks started, his voice halting. "Or I move with her."

"You move with her." Viola repeated, blankly. "Brooks, you've only known her for, like—"

"I know it's ridiculously soon." Brooks said. "But at some point, I have to grow up, right? I have to really take a chance and commit to something, and we get along really well—"

"I think it's a great idea." She cut him off. "I'll help you pack."

"Really?" Brooks looked up at her then, his face open and vulnerable.

She steeled herself and made the smile on her face just a little bit bigger. "Really."

Viola waved over the waitress. "Gin, please?" She turned to Brooks. "You want some?" When he shook his head no, she held up two fingers. "Make that a double for me, please!"

The waitress returned with her glass, and Viola downed it in one fluid motion. Brooks' eyes widened.

Viola slapped the table. "Whew!" She wiped her mouth with the back of her arm, feeling the warmth spread across her chest and up her neck.

"I'm grateful for the support?" Brooks' tone flipped up at the end of his sentence, making his statement sound more like a question. He still looked at Viola as though he wasn't sure what to make of her enthusiasm. "I've got to tell you, I was worried I'd get a lecture. Even my parents freaked out that we've only been together for such a short time. I thought you'd be so mad at me."

"No, no way. The Romance Queen is dead. Long live optimism!" Her voice was too loud, she could tell. She eyeballed the remnants of his beer. "You gonna finish that?"

Brooks looked warily at his drink as she grabbed it and swirled before draining the glass.

"Is everything okay?" He asked, concern filling his eyes.

She pulled out her phone and checked it. "Oh, man, I've gotta run. Wedding stuff with Ruby. You know I can't bail on that."

She stood up too quickly, her head spinning. Brooks stood up, too, his hand at her elbow, steadying her as she swayed slightly. "Seriously, are you okay, Reed?"

"Peachy! I'll be around to help you get started with the packing soon. I'll text you?"

"Sounds good," he said. The crease between his eyes had grown deeper with worry.

Viola saluted him, and an unexpected giggle escaped her lips. "Say hello to Emily for me!" she called as she swooped through the door.

The afternoon was painfully cold outside. The walk over to Ruby's place was short and uncomplicated, but Viola found herself staggering, walking near blind as she shielded her eyes from the too-bright sun. She felt her phone go off in her pocket. She pulled out the device, squinting and fumbling with the buttons as she tried to see who was contacting her.

FRANCINE.

Ugh. Viola pocketed the phone again. She knew that it had been too long since she'd sent any new drafts over to her agent. She'd seen Francesca's emails popping up in her inbox, friendly reminders that her deadline was coming up, just a week away, just a few days away... Had she hit it already? She rubbed the back of her neck, trying to remember what day it was now.

Her laptop had stayed closed with Matt at her house. The bay window was still shut. Viola couldn't remember the last time she had typed on a keyboard that wasn't on her phone. Her novel was feeling less and less important. It was a distant figment now, a vague idea of a story that sometimes popped up at the back of her head, but one which she could shut up with a beer or a glass of wine.

She turned onto Ruby's street. There was the perfect little house with the perfect little cherry blossom tree out front. Viola recognized Hannah's car parked out front, as well as Nadine's.

She let herself in through the front door. "Knock, knock!" She called. Her loud voice felt wrong in the quiet house.

Ruby popped her head around a corner. "Vi! We didn't think you'd be able to make it."

"I'm here for you, babe." Viola grinned and hopped over to her sister, slinging her arm around her shoulders. "Now where are those centerpieces? I'm about to decorate the heck out of a mason jar."

Ruby laughed nervously. Viola could feel her sister holding her just a little bit closer, propping her up against her body as they made their way down the hall. They found Hannah and Nadine in the kitchen, slaving away with glue guns and tiny pieces of creamsicle orange ribbon.

"Oh man, I missed out on the glue guns?" Viola whined. "I love wielding all that power."

"I still remember the decorations you 'helped with' at my weddin'," Hannah said with a laugh. "No way were we letting you near the craft supplies again."

Ruby settled Viola into a stool at the counter and handed her a mound of fake baby's breath. "You can arrange these," she instructed. "I need twenty small jars and three big vases."

"Sir, yes, sir." Viola nodded, picking up a handful of the plastic flowers.

Ruby turned to Hannah, her head cocking subtly in Viola's direction. "Should we crack out that cucumber water while we work?"

Hannah's eyebrows went up. She nodded in agreement. "Of course! So refreshing." She headed in the direction of the fridge.

Viola's pocket buzzed again. She pulled at it, letting the screen just barely peek out of her jeans. *FRANCINE*. She shoved it back in her pocket.

Nadine set down her centerpiece and opened up a cabinet to grab out a glass. She retrieved a bottle of red wine from near the sink and poured a few ounces. She held it up for Viola. "You might have missed the glue gun, but you came just in time for the par-tay." She giggled. "Ruby's been holding out on us with this cucumber water crap, but lucky for us I remember where she keeps the top shelf stuff."

"Oh, I don't think—" Ruby started.

Viola cut off the sounds of Ruby's objections by extending both her arms and waggling her fingers. "Gimme, gimme."

She took the glass and guzzled it down. She held it out again, catching Nadine before she could re-cork. "Hit me again, lady."

Ruby reached out a hand and started to take Viola's glass. "Slow down, we're just getting started." She laughed, the sound small and nervous.

"Trust me, I need this." Viola shakily pushed her sister's hand away and snatched up both the glass and the wine bottle. She poured herself a generous portion, throwing her head back to drain it again.

"That's enough, Vi." Ruby wasn't looking so demure

now. She took back the wine bottle, corked it, and set it on the kitchen table.

"God, stop judging me." Viola moaned. "It's been a long week, okay?" She snorted, realizing just how much of an understatement that was. "It's been a long *year*."

She stood up to grab the bottle, but this time Hannah blocked her path along with Ruby.

"You can talk to us," Hannah said. She reached out to take Viola's hand, giving it a little squeeze. "But you don't need any more to drink."

"You don't know what I need," Viola said. She could hear her voice getting nasty then, but it was hard to care. The haze had consumed her, no longer happy and dizzying, but heavy and pressing. She felt sick to her stomach. "None of you know what I need. *I* don't even know what I need."

She put both palms to her eyes, trying to block out the light and make the room stop spinning so violently. She turned back to her stool, reaching out for balance. The tears were coming before she could help herself. They were burning rivers down her cheeks and clotting her nose, making Viola feel as though she were choking.

"Vi?" Ruby asked, carefully putting a hand on her back. "You really don't look so—"

The churning wave in Viola's stomach slammed forward. She clutched at the countertop as she vomited all over stools and craft supplies, only narrowly missing the finished mason jars. She felt an instant relief from her nausea and dizziness from the room's incessant spinning, but with the moment of recovery came a terrifying, new sense of lucidity. She hadn't really been sobered up, but this was scary close. Her breaths came out ragged and desperate as she wiped her mouth, surveying the damage she'd done.

Viola turned back to the girls, who had been shocked

into silence. It was Ruby who found her composure first. She guided Viola forward and set her at a chair by the kitchen table. She glided around the countertop, whisking undecorated mason jars out of harm's way and using a kitchen rag to start sopping up the mess. Then she opened up a cabinet, retrieving another glass and filling it with water from the sink. She returned to the girls at the table and offered it up to Viola.

"Here. Drink."

Viola took the water hesitantly, sipping it in slow, small swallows.

Ruby's calm demeanor unsettled her sister. This was a far cry from the night her muslin mockup had been ruined. It was even a difference from all the times that Viola had felt Ruby's eyes on her, watching her drink more and more at each wedding and party. This was scarier.

"Ladies, do you mind grabbing something new for Vi to wear? You can get anything from my closet."

Hannah and Nadine nodded. They disappeared, leaving the sisters alone.

"Roo, I—"

"It's okay." Ruby cut her off. "Really, it's... it's okay."

"You have every right to be mad." Viola said. "I've been going off the deep-end lately. I've got this deadline I haven't written anything for. Matt moved back in. And—" She hesitated, wishing for a moment that she could have the alcohol-induced haze back rather than this stark feeling of sick clarity. "And Brooks is moving with Emily. To Charlotte."

Ruby's eyes grew wide and sympathetic. "To Charlotte?"

Viola nodded miserably. "I'm in over my head."

Her sister took the water glass and set it on the table. She pulled Viola close, hugging her to her chest. "I want to help you," she said. "That's what family is for."

"I don't know what to do," Viola said. She could hear the desperation in her voice. The pathetic whine. "I don't know what I want or how to fix things. I don't know how to get control."

Ruby stroked her hair. "Well, I know one way," she said, her voice quiet. "Consider yourself relieved of Maid of Honor duties. I can have Nadine or Hannah take over. She's got more time now that she's finally taken that honeymoon. You can just relax. Enjoy the wedding instead of having to plan it."

Viola sat up, the sick feeling returning to her stomach once more. "Ruby, you can't be serious."

"I've been thinking about it for a while. I think this is for the best." Ruby continued to stroke Viola's hair, but she wasn't looking her sister in the eye.

All at once, Viola felt as though she would be sick again. She clutched at the countertop, her knuckles turning white from her grip. She knew that this decision would not have come easy for Ruby, but Viola had pushed her to it. Driven her to the edge with her reckless behavior.

But the worst thing, the thing that was making the wine sour in her stomach and her head pulse with pain, was the fact that Viola had absolutely no idea how to recover from all this. She was in too deep. She didn't even know what she wanted anymore.

"Why don't you head home?" Ruby asked gently, rubbing her back. "I'll see you at the Gunter wedding tomorrow night, right?"

Viola nodded, miserable. Just what she needed. Another wedding.

Chapter 18

Viola went into the Gunter wedding sober. It had taken some real effort.

Now that she was removed from the immediacy of her dependency, she was surprised to find how much she had been leaning into the haze. How much she had been trying to drown out her life. She had slipped so far into the fog that she hadn't realized when her whole world had gone black.

She'd spent a Wednesday night clearing out her fridge. The glass bottles had clanked in the black garbage bag as she'd taken it to the apartment complex trash cans. The sound was like ecstasy, making Viola feel like one of Pavlov's salivating dogs as she had to resist digging back into the trash bag before dumping the contents into the massive bin.

When she'd returned to her apartment, she'd found Matt on the couch flipping through TV channels and drumming his fingers on the coffee table like he was leading a full band. The sound grated on her ears. Especially now that she was sober enough to hear every note. An old *Star Trek* rerun was on. Matt had skipped over it in favor of *Transformers*, barely watching the TV as he drummed those fingers louder. Viola hadn't bothered to sit down next to him.

Instead, she had found her old spot at her desk. She pulled the blinds for the bay window, letting the deep blue of the evening settle into the untouched corners of her apartment. She ran her fingers over the frayed edges of her spiral notebook. It had felt right.

She'd opened up her laptop. The familiar tones of it starting up had given her a little rush, and for the first time that evening, she stopped salivating over the beer in the trash can and started to focus her attentions elsewhere. Duncan had hopped up onto her lap, his small orange body nestling in deep as she wrote. She'd gotten a chapter in when she'd felt Matt's hand on her shoulder, asking if she'd put the laptop away to come watch something with him.

All of that effort was finally beginning to pay off now. Viola sat at her table at the Gunter wedding, water in hand instead of wine. Unfortunately, in the dim, purple lights of the reception, the old ache for a drink was coming back. Polished glasses sparkled as couples moved from table to table, and the sounds of the bartenders mixing themed cocktails landed on Vi's ears like a waterfall.

Matt had been acting antsy all evening, his fingers now tapping out their frantic beat on his suit pants. It was making Viola crazy. She itched to be anywhere else, away from his palpable energy.

She scanned the crowd for an escape and immediately spotted Brooks and Emily. Emily was dressed in pink chiffon, a dreamy little number with a sweetheart neckline. It was a perfect complement to the classic tuxedo Brooks wore, complete with his own pink bow tie.

Brooks was energetic and cheery, dancing with a toddler

who wore braided pigtails and a massive smile. The girl stood on his feet, giggling as he walked her up and down to the beat. He looked happy, relaxed. Watching him dance with the girl felt like a privilege. Like Viola was spying in on some intimate part of Brooks, a part that he reserved for the sweetest, most tender of company.

Emily tapped him on the shoulder, cutting in to steal him away and off to a table together. Brooks waved goodbye to the little girl, who looked disappointed by his having to leave. But he blew her a kiss as he walked away, and all her frustration melted, leaving the toddler grinning and waggling her fingers back. Emily swooped between the two of them, her long flowy dress hitting the girl's face as she ushered Brooks up and away.

Of course they would be at this wedding. Viola hadn't texted Brooks since the day they had lunch together, but she should have guessed. She'd seen his messages come through, each one consciously ignored but still needling at the back of her brain.

"Hey, it's your friend." Matt stood up a bit too fast from where he sat behind Viola and waved over at the couple. It was a relief not to hear the drumming fingers anymore. He put a hand on Viola's shoulder. His fingers were damp with sweat, making her grimace. She shimmied away the slightest bit as Brooks and Emily made their way through the crowd to join them at their table.

"Hey!" Emily waved, smiling broadly. "Good to see some familiar faces."

"Here, come take our seats." Matt offered. "I was just about to whisk Viola out to the dance floor."

Matt pulled her close. Brooks smiled at them, the barest curl in the corners of his mouth. He started to take Matt's seat when Emily elbowed him to stay standing. "Let's go, too! I love this song."

Emily took Brooks' hand as the first notes of *Beauty and the Beast*'s title song came out loud and warbly over the sound system. The couples walked together out onto the dance floor, with Viola sending a wincing Brooks a small apologetic smile as Angela Lansbury's ancient voice blasted out the opening lines.

They didn't stay together long, though. Matt twirled Viola across the floor, pulling her close to his body as the music really took over. He rested his forehead on hers, closing his eyes and breathing deeply.

"Viola..." he murmured, his voice low and shaking. The sweat had picked up on his brow. "These past few weeks together have been like a dream."

She tried to listen. But Brooks danced with Emily on the other side of the floor, his fingertips gently cradling her smooth tanned hand in his own. Viola couldn't look away. She couldn't begin to think of anything else, and Matt's words were barely a whisper in the back of her mind.

She remembered the way that Brooks smelled, spicy and warm. She wondered what it felt like to be Emily now, breathing him in and getting lost in the aura. Her heart jumped in her chest, pulling her away, floating her over to him.

"There's something I've been wanting to ask you," Matt was saying. "It never felt right to ask again before now. But now things are changing. Maybe... maybe this time you're ready."

"Hmm?"

Brooks had leaned forward to whisper something in Emily's ear. Her face had split into a smile and she playfully pushed him on the shoulder.

His eyes caught Viola's then. She could feel her face burning and instinct told her to look away, to turn back to Matt. But she didn't. She held his gaze, watching him dance with Emily's body molded to his. Only a few feet apart but a million miles away. He smiled at her from across the floor. There was something about the expression that didn't reach his eyes. What was that look? Was he trying to tell her something?

"Viola." Matt's body had stopped swaying. He grasped her elbows, pulling her back to really look at her.

She tore her gaze away from the couple across the dance floor. Matt looked so earnest.

"I want to try again. I still have this and it's only for you." His voice was a nervous whisper as he pulled a familiar black box out of his pocket. Viola's breath caught in her throat. "Be with me. We're good for each other. Just think about how much you've changed in the past few weeks. It just feels like you've really committed to me above all else. I think it's time."

The music shifted as Viola took a step back. She understood then: Matt's sweat, his shaky voice. How had she missed all the signs? Her stomach churned, and she ached to race for the bar and drown herself in a drink. She ran her hands through her hair, trying to steady herself with a distraction as she looked anywhere but into Matt's ardent eyes.

Say something. Say anything! This was what she wanted. Stable Matt. Reliable Matt. Committed Matt. Someone who was good for Viola, who made her into her best self.

But that was the rub, wasn't it?

Viola knew it then, all in one painful flash. Matt was making her over, for sure. But it wasn't into her best self. It was into someone else entirely. She had stopped writing and ignored her deadlines at his behest. She was more serious, less funny and clever. She was unchallenged and unmotivated, and she was burying herself in the bottom of a bottle to forget about those facts.

But she was coming out of the cloud now, regaining her sobriety through her own willpower and fighting to get back her life. It was helping her to see things as they really were. She was growing up and realizing what she really wanted and needed.

Matt was a good man. He just wasn't her man. And, worst of all, Viola knew exactly who was. And she had let him slip away.

Matt was still waiting on an answer. He cradled the tiny box in his fingers, clearly eager to open it up and reveal the ring that Viola could remember from the time before. She put a hand out, stopping him from opening it. She opened her mouth to speak, having absolutely no idea what she would possibly say.

A hand touched her shoulder. "Can I cut in?"

She turned. Brooks stood behind her, smiling at the pair of them, oblivious to what he had interrupted. "Reed and I have made swing dancing a bit of a tradition, and when the music calls for it…"

Matt started to interrupt, lifting the ring box to gesture. Viola felt the panic rise in her chest. She was trapped. She could face Matt's inevitable question and let down a good man because they simply weren't the best match or—maybe worse—face Brooks, the man who had shown her what love could really look like before she'd squandered her chance to have it with him.

"I can't take no for an answer," Brooks said with a small smile, taking Viola's hand before she or Matt could say anything in reply. He pulled her through the crowd and away. It took every fiber of her being to push down the shiver that danced across her skin.

He led her to the center of the floor, and Viola tried her best not to look back at where Matt still stood holding his box. Gosh, she really wished that she had a drink now.

Chapter 19

The swing dance was over far too soon. Brooks and Viola separated after one final spin, panting. He wiped some sweat from his brow. His curly mop of hair had fallen out of its perfect coif down into his eyes, and Brooks had to run his fingers through the coils, taming them into some semblance of refinement.

"I think this might be as good as it gets." He laughed. A slow, rhythmic Ed Sheeran song began to play over the loudspeakers. Brooks smiled and extended a hand to Viola. "Dare you be seen with me for another dance?"

Viola's eyes darted across the dance floor, searching for Matt. She saw him standing at the edge of the crowd, still holding his little box and beginning to look impatient. Her stomach flipped, and she grabbed Brooks' hand firmly, starting the dance before she would have to finally confront Matt.

Brooks pulled her close, his hands finding their way to her waist. She put her own hands on his shoulders and looked up. He was watching Matt, too, his brow knotted.

"Am I keeping you away from your date for too long? Matt looks eager to have you back."

Viola's voice caught in her throat. "He's... well, to be honest, I think I just made the choice to avoid him... I feel like a monster." She could feel tears pricking her eyes. She didn't want to hurt Matt again, but she knew she wasn't ready to face his hopeful eyes and nervous hands.

She couldn't say what compelled her to admit as much to Brooks. There was just something easy with him, something that made her want to spill it all, every last painful, drunken detail of the past few weeks without him.

"Old habits die hard?" Brooks raised an eyebrow.

"Something like that..." She admitted. She paused, the words just on the tip of her tongue. "He proposed to me. Again."

Brooks' eyes widened, the dark pupils flickering. Viola could feel his grip on her waist tighten ever so slightly. He cleared his throat and set his shoulders, his serious gaze lost somewhere in the crowd. "And what did you say?"

"God, I don't know. You pulled me away to dance with you before I could answer." She wondered if she felt as miserable as she looked.

Brooks looked back at her then. Her mind jumped to another moment shared between them, when he had told her that he was moving to Charlotte with Emily. His eyes were just as searching, just as vulnerable as Viola's had been then. It was clear to her that he was asking a question of her now. It was something intangible. Something he felt too deeply to put into words.

Finally, she broke his gaze, her eyes fixing on their shoes. What could she possibly say in this moment that would make things the way they ought to be? Brooks was happy with Emily. Viola was supposed to be happy with Matt. All was going well in their lives. Everything was on the right trajectory. Why would she mess that up now?

And just as she had responded to the news of Brooks' move, he responded in kind to this unspoken test between them. He loosened up his grip and started to step away. "I think maybe I should be getting back—"

She stepped forward, stopping him with a hand on his wrist. "Can we just finish this dance? I can answer Matt after. He's already waited this long."

Brooks took a deep breath and returned to his position. His hands settled back at Viola's waist. An instinct she could no longer fight took her closer to him, so his chest just grazed her own. She rested her head on his shoulder, breathing in the deep, heady scent that she had been imagining all night. They danced that way for most of the song. His body responded in perfect rhythm to her own.

A phrase she'd written a thousand times before appeared in her mind's eye: they were alone in a crowded room. What a cliché. She shuffled aside, trying to position herself to block Matt's view of Brooks' comfortable body. She was already acting the monster, but she couldn't let him be wounded by a sight like that.

Brooks cleared his throat again, and she pulled back to look at him as he spoke. "You know it's silly; for a while, I thought that there might be something between the two of us."

Viola felt that twist in her gut again. This time it felt like a knife. "That's not silly. I, um, actually thought there might be something there, too. For a minute."

He looked surprised, one eyebrow raising the slightest bit. "I thought you looked so pretty that night we met, but nope. Called me right out for my pickup line." He laughed, but his eyes showed something more.

"It was a bad pickup line," Viola admitted, permitting a small smile. "You'd think that with all your practice, you'd have a classier opening."

"Ah, your biting snark never fails to charm me." He smiled at her then, his eyes shining and bright. "Same goes for your bitter wedding jokes and stories about letting Duncan eat Ben and Jerrys right out of your bowl. It was like catnip for single men."

They both laughed at that one. Silence settled in between them as Brooks searched her gaze, the lines on his forehead wrinkling up in his focus. No more talk of jokes or super-powers.

"That day? At my family's barbecue?" Viola knew then that they were thinking about the same thing, the same moment. She could see the yellow and white kitchen in clear focus, with its worn-out cabinets and faded height marker. Brooks' eyes were wracked with emotion as he gave voice to her thoughts. "I almost kissed you. Can you believe that?"

"No." Viola could barely hear her own voice. "It's unbelievable."

"I think you would have slapped me and then called me out for making you live through a cliché." He smiled at her.

"God, Brooks. I'm sorry I've been so cynical." She shuffled, trying not to sound as pathetic as she felt. Her hair swooped forward into her eyes, and she let it hide her face. "I'm starting to learn that maybe a cliché isn't the worst thing in the world. Maybe those romantic gestures have become clichés because they're, well... they're pretty darn romantic. I'm just sorry I've been so biting and harsh."

Brooks laughed. The sound took her by surprise. He smiled down at her. "Are you kidding? That's what I love about you, Reed." He pushed the hair out of her eyes, tucking the thick black lock behind her ear.

And just like that, there it was again: electricity.

She felt that now familiar stirring in her chest, something soft and fluttering. The heat at the back of her neck flamed out to the rest of her body, sending sparking tingles through her fingers and toes. *Physical touch tricks the brain into creating a sense of intimacy.* She didn't care; she invited it.

Viola leaned forward as the music swelled. She was so close to him—

"Brooks, I broke a heel."

Viola snapped around to see Emily standing barefoot behind her, shoes in hand. She jumped, instantly pulling her hands from Brooks'.

"I need to run back to the house," Emily continued. Was there something in her eyes? What did she think that she'd seen? "Hey, Vi, are you still coming over next weekend to help us pack? I told Brooks that I needed a woman's touch to help me organize my jewelry collection."

"Ah, yes." Viola stepped further back from Brooks, tucking her hands safely by her sides. "That is what I'm known for. My womanly touch."

The joke came out awkward and stilted. Viola's heart was still pounding in her ears. She slipped her hands into her dress pockets, twisting the fabric inside. Calm down.

"Let's start kind of early, so we can get a jump on things before the humidity really kicks in. Sound good?" Emily smiled.

Viola nodded. She turned back to Brooks, who had busied himself with a piece of lint on his suit jacket. Whatever moment that was shared between them, it was over now and there was no retrieving it. "I guess I had better be getting back then."

"Yeah," Brooks said, finally looking up. "I think Matt is probably pretty anxious to get an answer from you."

"Ooh, an answer?" Emily's eyes lit up, and she leaned closer to their little group. "Wait—did Matt *propose*?"

Viola tried to answer, but the words weren't coming out. She settled for shrugging and giving a little half-smile. Emily's face exploded into a grin and she smooshed Viola into a hug. "Congratulations! You have to invite us back for the wedding."

"Course," she mumbled. She looked over at Brooks again, who still wasn't meeting her eyes.

"Yeah," he agreed with Emily, gaze fixed on the floor. "Invite us back for the wedding."

Viola saw Matt crossing the dance floor, the little box tucked by his side. There was no avoiding it now. She'd have to face him.

Emily leaned forward to kiss her on the cheek and wave goodbye. Brooks raised two fingers, the barest wave in her direction. Viola watched them disappear together into the crowd of guests.

Chapter 20

The storm had started shortly after the Gunter wedding.

Matt and Viola had retreated to the car they had come in and, even though she had the rain as an excuse for her silence, he must have intuited that her news would not be good. The storm had come down in a deluge, great, gray, dirty drops splattering across the windshield like broken bullets. In the fading light of the evening, the rain outside left streaks of shadow on Matt's face. Viola hadn't been able to tell if he was crying.

"So that's it then?" He had asked her. His voice was unsteady. Imprecise. "*Again*, Viola? You pull this on me again?"

"I'm sorry," she pled with him. Her heart hurt. "I never meant to—"

"Of course, you didn't mean to!" He threw his hands up, exasperated. "You didn't mean to break my heart. Twice! You didn't mean to make me look like a fool. You didn't mean to take advantage of my feelings."

"Matt, I—"

"I, I, I. It's always about you, Viola, about what *you* want. You want the nonsensical career in writing. The impractical hours and habits. You're *selfish!*"

His voice rang out on the last word, hovering between them in the quiet of the car.

As soon as he said it, Matt looked as though some weight had been lifted. He'd finally given voice to the problem that had always been between them, the thing that had kept them from being something great together. He was a great guy. He was going to be a real catch for somebody.

But Viola just wasn't that girl.

Matt ran a hand through his hair, taking deep breaths. Vi could see the slow return of the Southern gentleman as he sat up straight and stared at the steering wheel.

"What now?" He asked quietly. "I mean, are you going to chase after him, or do I just have the pleasure of looking like the cuckold without you actually leaving me for anyone?"

"Um, no." She had shifted in her seat. The evening was growing colder, and she could see her breath even in the car, releasing in sad puffs that fogged the windows. "I don't think I *can* go after him. I think Emily might be his person. I can't get in the way of that."

"We're talking about the same Emily, right?" Matt raised an eyebrow in her direction and with the shift of his face, she could see that his eyes were hard and cold. Viola could feel the tears in her own eyes, and she willed back the sting with all the force she could muster. Matt rolled his eyes. "Jeez, Viola, it can't end like this. Forget your stupid romance novel crap for a second and think about reality for once. You're really going to break up with me because of him and then not try to go after him at all?"

He looked at her silently and then started up the car to take her home. It wasn't forgiveness. But it was something close. It was the closest thing they could get after the relationship they had endured together.

Nevertheless, she didn't know how to respond to him. She couldn't ruin what Brooks had with Emily. He seemed happy. He was moving for her, for crying out loud!

When she didn't respond for a long time, Matt took off out of the parking lot, and they made the slow drive through the downpour back to her apartment in silence. She rested her head on the cool window, closing her eyes and willing herself to any place other than this.

Matt packed his things back up that night. The Beer Hunter t-shirt. The new toothbrush. By midnight, all the remnants of his life with Viola were completely gone.

At first, she didn't know what to do with herself. She paced her tiny apartment, desperate for distraction. Fighting down her increasing agitation, she had raided her cabinets, opened them all up to search for bottles that she knew were no longer there. She was sweating. Her heart beat too fast. Briefly—only briefly—she considered braving the rain to make a run for the 24-hour convenience store. She thought better of it as the lightning outside ripped a white hot tear in the Atlanta sky.

So Viola was forced to make do with her new sobriety and her new feelings. She steeled her mind and straightened her back. She would just have to make do. She would have to start over the only way she knew how.

She marched to her bedroom and put on her softest sweatpants and t-shirt. She tied her long, black hair into the familiar top knot. She scooped up Duncan from his cozy cat bed, ignoring his annoyed mews to cuddle him close under her chin. Her heart still pounded, but his soft fur on her skin soothed the beating.

Last of all, she opened the blinds to the bay window

once more. Even in the gray light of the early morning hours, the city skyline was an instant comfort to her. With her apartment lights off, the distant billboards and office floodlights lit her room the faintest yellow. The rain was still coming down, drenching her window with cleansing rivulets. Atlanta stood tall and proud, its buildings reaching up, up, up through the storm to tempt the lightning.

Viola cracked her window the barest amount before sitting down at her desk chair. She liked the way that the rain hammered out an unpredictable pattern on the glass. It was almost enough to drown out the beating of her heart. A fine mist crept in through the crack in the window, cooling the room and making Duncan cuddle closer.

Some ancient habit—unbroken despite Matt's intervention—compelled her to pull open her desk drawer. Viola was surprised to realize just how long it had been since she'd had it open. She picked up her Whitman collection and carefully set it out of the way before she rummaged through old papers, pulling out various plot outlines and cashed checks. It was her whole identity, captured in ink and paper, crammed away. Had she really allowed herself to forget this part of her life? She felt oddly exposed and vulnerable then, as though some buried part of herself was finally being given the chance to breathe again. Eventually she found the rubber band bound stack she sought.

She placed Duncan down on the top of her closed laptop, where he curled into a donut shape and settled in once more. Hesitant and the oddest bit nervous, she took off the rubber band and pulled out the first piece of paper. She slumped into her office chair and listened to the rain pound as she read.

Dear Miss Reed,

Last year, I lost my husband, Arnold. We had been married

for thirty years. For the longest time after, I didn't know what to do with myself. My children keep pushing me to date men at my church. My grandkids are trying to teach me about something called Zoom. None of it interested me. In fact, nothing at all interested me until I read your book, Midnight Magic. I could swear it was written about my Arnold...

Viola placed the letter down next to Duncan and thumbed to another.

To Viola Reed,

My name is Remi Pope. I'm thirteen. We had to read a book for Mrs. Robinson's seventh grade English class, and I chose yours. It was so awesome! Noah was just like this guy in Algebra, Nate Hansen...

Viola placed it down and found more.

Miss Reed.

My new friend Viola.

To whom it may concern.

To the best author EVER!!!

It was the first time that Viola had read any of her fan letters without a hint of distaste or cynicism. Much to her surprise, she found herself enjoying them just as much as she had when she read them the first time. Maybe more. Now she understood better where these people were coming from.

The rain kept coming for days after and Viola kept reading. She'd sit at the bay window, lights off in her apartment, and take in the letters by the glow of the city skyline. When Duncan would mew, she would walk to the kitchen and get him snacks. When she was hungry, she would eat. But otherwise, it was all reading all the time. She consumed years' worth of letters, letting the hunger for more consume her until her entire world was just rain, and writing, and stories of romance.

Of course, life went on outside of her window. She got messages from Brooks, reminding her about the promise she'd made to come help him pack. She couldn't bring herself to respond, though. Every time that she'd see his name pop up on her screen, she would feel that familiar ache in her heart. It was back to reading as quick as she could, losing herself in any love story other than her own.

The calendar date they had set for packing came and went. Viola couldn't bring herself to say goodbye, so she kept on sitting by the bay window. She kept on reading. Brooks was gone, moved out of the city, out of the state, and soon to be out of her mind. And there was no getting him back.

Ruby and Hannah both expressed their concerns when Vi didn't come round for so long. They stopped by her house without warning, bringing desserts and 80s rom-com movies. Much to their surprise, Viola had welcomed their company. She took her only breaks from her reading to turn on the living room light and bring them in. They sat on her couch, chatting about Ruby's fast-approaching wedding and Hannah's married life. Viola told them about Matt, and they comforted her in all the right ways.

And when those conversations were over, they kept sitting, and talking, and laughing. The trio was transported to another time in their lives, when the world was simpler and boys still had cooties. They reminisced for hours and ate entirely too much chocolate, and they watched strangers struggle with umbrellas and puddles in the rain outside Vi's window.

Viola read them some of her letters. It was the first time that she'd told anyone about her fan mail at all, much less opened up this deeply intimate part of herself. Ruby and Hannah responded better than she could ever have dreamed. They laughed with her. They made some of the same jokes that she had thought to herself the first time she'd read the letters, mostly about teenage fantasies or desperate housewives.

The girls also voiced their agreement with the letters, though. Viola hadn't expected that. Ruby admitted to reading *Hour of Ecstasy* during her break at work. Hannah, cheeks aflame with blush, confessed that *The Time is Now* had provided some inspiration on her honeymoon with Aaron. They had read every page Viola had ever written, and they loved them all. The letters had nailed it.

When the rain finally stopped at the end of the week, Viola felt like a new person. She still had an ache deep inside. She still thought about Brooks when his name would pop up on her phone screen again. But with the cleansing storm, she had gained her own new perspective. It had washed her doubts and concerns away to uncover the raw emotion beneath that she was now willing to embrace.

She thought of Hannah and Ruby and all the other women reading her stories, looking for a little escape. Looking for their own small love story. And, in an instant, she felt inspiration again. It was an electricity that came from deep inside of her, as authentic and vibrant as the sparks she had felt when Brooks had touched her skin. She knew exactly what she wanted to write. *Screw "trite."* Francine could eat her heart out.

Viola kept the bay window open as the world dried around her. The sun pierced through the clouds, triumphantly shooting rays into her little living room. She relished in it as she sat at her desk once more and opened her laptop to start typing.

The title page came first, with which she took some stylistic liberties:

~~Single.~~

~~Taken.~~

Completely Undatable.

Viola sat back, crossing her arms with satisfaction as she toyed with an idea for her first line.

Okay, so her hero Walt Whitman might not have ever written a piece with a title like that. But it felt good. It felt right. It felt like, for the first time in a long time, Viola was a *real* writer, working on a story that meant something and brought out the best of her abilities. She was more than a quantity-pusher or someone who only wrote to the lowest common denominator. She was contributing to something greater than herself.

The characters were already completely formed in her head. The plot was hammered out. And, like a million times before, she knew that in penning this new love story that she could right the wrongs of romance.

She began with a description of her protagonist: a young woman. Professional. Cynical. Long black hair and dark eyes—romance novel rules about minorities be damned. A great love for orange tabby cats.

Waiting in the back of her mind to make his entrance from across a crowded dance floor was her romantic lead. He was a playboy. A little immature and cocky. Nothing like the Jean-Lucs or Marks or Benoits she had written before.

He was even better.

CHAPTER 21

SPRING

"Well, it's not exactly a sequel."

"I know," Viola admitted, twirling the long cord of her phone as she paced her apartment.

"I mean, maybe in the way that those Batman movies with Clooney and Keaton and Kilmer were sequels. Loose."

"Might I also remind you it's late."

"I know," Viola repeated.

"Like, you'd be blacklisted with any other agent, late."

Viola's stomach was a tight, heavy ball of anticipation. "Spit it out, Fran. Are you calling my book a Clooney Batman?"

On the other side of the line, she could hear her agent sucking the remnants of her morning mocha through a loud straw. Viola held her breath. And finally — "It's a home run, sweetie. Knocked it outta the park. Think Christian Bale Batman."

Viola held the phone to her chest as she jumped in the air and pumped her fists. Duncan got spooked, hissing at her as he retreated to his safe space by the kitchen cabinet full of treats.

"I can't say if I'm more surprised that you liked my new approach or that you know who Christian Bale is." Viola laughed.

"I'm going to pretend that you didn't just insult my worldly knowledge and assure you that your book will undoubtedly do well. If you can keep producing like this, your career might just have a second life."

"Thank you," Viola said. "Truly."

"You're welcome," Francine replied. "But I do feel the need to remind you that if you keep me waiting on work for months at a time with nary an email to satisfy me, I will hire the finest bounty hunters the east coast has to offer to draw and quarter you. It will be a warning to procrastinators the world over."

Vi could hear the smile in Francine's voice and picture her now, cheetah pumps propped up on her desk and arms folded in satisfaction. It was funny—she'd gotten approval from Fran a million times before. She'd launched her profession, after all. But this time, this instance where she'd written from the heart and put her soul out there in paper and ink, this felt like she'd finally won her over.

"I'm proud of ya, kid." Francine confirmed her thoughts.

"Can you tell me that one more time?" Vi teased. "Just so I can replay the sound of it over in my dreams tonight?"

"You already got me choked up and my mascara misting. I will suffer no more indignities today."

"Viola, you didn't."

Ruby's bridal shower was held one week before her wedding. It was late, of course, as was to be expected, what with a former Maid of Honor who didn't have a clue about organization or planning. Nadine had to scramble to do the planning, begging Vi for contacts she didn't have and seeing who could cater on such short notice. But in the end, the party was splendid.

All the girls from Viola's hometown were there. They'd brought big bags bursting with home goods and romantic baubles. They drank fruity cocktails under pastel banners and giggled together as they caught up on gossip. Ruby looked like she was floating; the smile hadn't left her face all day. She'd greeted each guest with the same exuberance, shaking their hands and hugging them like it was the first time she'd seen them in years.

The biggest smile, though, had been reserved for this moment, when Ruby opened her sister's gift. It was a smaller package, a plain brown box tied with a simple pink ribbon. It didn't look like much. But when Ruby undid the wrapping and pulled out the tiny framed paper, Viola knew that she had found a winner.

"I can't accept this, Vi." Ruby flashed the poem to her guests before turning it back to her. Her long, thin fingers delicately swept the glass as she re-read the poem line by line under her breath. Her twisting blonde curls swooped forward to obscure her face, but not before her sister could see that her eyes had welled with tears.

"I figured it can be your something borrowed," Viola explained, stepping forward. "It's also old. The framer gave me a lot of grief about how delicate it was before he started the project. And it's blue, I guess. Because it's a sad poem."

"I know what *Once I Pass'd Through a Populous City* is about." Ruby smiled and cradled the poem against her chest. She turned to her guests to explain. "It's a love poem by Walt Whitman. A man is set on remembering everything about a city he visits, but it all fades away because the only thing he can remember about it is the woman he loves.

They don't stay together forever, but she always stays in his heart."

The women sighed and offered a few claps. Nadine returned to the gift pile to grab the next box. Ruby grabbed Viola's sleeve, pulling her close.

"Vi, this is a perfect wedding gift." She said. "But I really can't accept this. What if it gets lost in the wedding shuffle? It's too important to you."

"It won't get lost," Viola assured her. "I took the liberty of hiring out some help for your big day to keep things clean and organized."

Ruby started to object to the gesture, but Viola held up a finger and continued. "I talked to your planner, too, about hanging this somewhere in your dressing room so that you can see it. I took care of that when I spoke with her about the mason jars. And I know you thought that chrysanthemums wouldn't be possible this time of year, but it turns out I have a florist in my building who grows them in his shop year-round."

"Vi..." Ruby's eyes were wide and curious. Her brow had knitted together, creasing softly in the middle as she tried to figure her sister out.

They were interrupted by Nadine, who was clearing her throat and offering up the next gift. Ruby set the frame aside delicately and took the new box.

Viola slipped back into the crowd of guests, allowing herself to disappear as the women *oohed* and *ahhed* over the next round of crock pots and dinner plates. She found Hannah at the kitchen counter, munching on tea cakes and working her way through a drink.

"Want some?" Hannah offered, extending her hand for Viola to take a sip.

Vi hesitated. She could feel that old, familiar thirst burning at the back of her throat. She willed it down.

"I'm good," she said. "I, uh, I stopped drinking. I actually threw out all my bottles before the Gunter wedding."

Hannah raised an eyebrow and put a hand on her hip. "Who is this woman?" She teased. "Don't worry, it's just Sprite. You can still have some if you'd like." She took another bite of tea cake and moaned. "And you definitely have to try some of these. I've had, like, six."

"Six tea cakes?" Viola laughed and elbowed her friend. "Dang, lady, someone's planning on gaining that first year of marriage fifteen."

"Yeah, about that..." Hannah smiled, resting one hand delicately on her belly.

Viola's eyes widened. "You are *not!*"

"Just found out a few days ago." Hannah grinned. "It wasn't planned, but we're so happy. And it turns out, I don't get sick—I get *starvin'*."

"Aaron must be freaking out."

"He's already painted our spare room. Twice."

Viola laughed. "Full dad mode."

She reached out and grabbed her friend's hand, smiling softly. Could it really have only been a few months ago when she was worrying about losing her to Aaron at their wedding? The thought felt silly now. Things were changing so fast that she didn't have time anymore to think about how she might be affected.

This, this was a very good thing. Hannah would make a great mom. And just like that, Viola could envision Ruby taking that next step, too. Giving her some sweet little niece or nephew to chase around the playground. The thought surprised Viola with how happy it made her.

She was surprised to feel Hannah squeeze her hand. She cocked her head at Viola, blue eyes sparkling. "Talk to me about what's going on in your world these days. Don't get me wrong—I like this Viola. The one who is sober, and writes again, and gossips with her friends. But you seem like something's a little off. Is there somethin' going on that I should know about?"

"Of course not," Viola assured her. "Life is totally great. I finished my book. Did I already tell you that?"

"Wow, congratulations."

"Yep," Viola continued. "Submitted it over to Francine last weekend. She loved it. So nothing to complain about over here."

"Nothin' at all?" Hannah asked innocently, stealing another sip of her Sprite. "Have you informed the inspiration behind your book about the success of his love story?"

Viola could feel her stomach souring. She rubbed at the back of her neck, trying to tame the heat she felt spreading there. "Han, come on. He moved to Charlotte. He's with Emily. He seems happy. I can't do that to him. I can't ruin things."

"You were good for him, Vi." Hannah said. "I know I made my jokes about Hardly Committed Hardison, but even I'll admit that you two were a decent match. And after what Aaron was telling me about what Brooks went through back in college, I definitely think you were what he needed—"

"I'm sorry, what?" Viola was puzzled. "What did Brooks go through in college?"

"Come on, you guys had to have talked about Chelsea. Apparently she was a big deal."

"Oh, yeah, of course." Viola nodded. She could remember the somber way Brooks had spoken about her. The way he hadn't been able to meet her eyes. "But everyone goes through bad breakups. It doesn't mean that we're destined to be with the next person who comes along and shows us a little attention. Emily is way better for him than me."

Hannah shook her head. "But it wasn't just a breakup, right? I mean, she got pregnant. He thought it was his, but then it turned out to be his fraternity brother's kid. That's *rough*."

Viola's head was spinning. Her mind flashed back to Brooks, holding Wyatt at the barbecue. Brooks, dancing with a little girl at the Gunter wedding. Brooks, teasing about finding his "Mama Duggar" to give him eight children. Her stomach felt sick. "He just told me that Chelsea wanted him to be someone else."

"Yeah, I guess she wanted him to be his fraternity brother," Hannah said dryly. "Sounds like Chelsea did a real number on him."

"I can't believe he never told me all that." Viola shook her head in disbelief. She braced herself on the kitchen counter, feeling more than a little dizzy. "Emily doesn't want kids. She's made that abundantly clear."

"And Brooks does?"

"It's all he wants," Viola told her. "You should see him with his nephew. He gets all paternal and doting and can't take his eyes off the kid. It's really pretty cute; he's like *obsessed*—"

Viola cut off, realizing that she was getting away from herself. Hannah crossed her arms and shook her head, clearly suppressing a massive smile. She was the picture of coy and coquettish, sipping her Sprite with wide eyes that made a farce of innocence.

"Uh-huh." She clucked condescendingly. "Well then. I'd say that what Brooks needs now is someone who has had time to figure out what she wants. Someone who won't fall for cheap romance or some Don Juan fraternity brother because she knows what love really is. Someone who would give him those kids when she's good and ready, and he'd never have any doubts about who she is or what he means to her."

Hannah took Viola's hand once more, holding it to her chest. "You deserve to be happy, too," she told Vi, her voice going soft and all sense of teasing fading away.

"But come on, Han. *Me?* In some grand, steal back my man, fairy tale gesture? That's so—"

"Cliché," Hannah agreed, smiling. "Sure. And I know you're afraid of those. I know your parents let you down and made you swear off love and all things that reminded you of it. And maybe romance really is something that your parents didn't deserve, but *you do*. So take a chance. Take a chance on *him*."

The girls were interrupted by the sound of more clapping. They turned to see Ruby unboxing another present. She pulled out a massive headboard, her face lighting up.

"Thank you, Diana!" She proclaimed. "I never thought anyone would actually pick this off the registry."

Hannah nudged Viola and offered her a little plate with a tea cake. "Try one, they're good." She said. "And then cowboy up, and go chase your man. Because no girl who casually references the Kardashians is destined to be Brooks Hardison's 'Mama Duggar.'"

Viola laughed but couldn't concentrate. Her mind was in a frenzy as she thought of Brooks now. Was he happy in Charlotte? Was he satisfied? Had she just messed things up with him for the thousandth time?

Her eyes drifted over to where her little framed poem stood, propped against the box that it came in. She thought of its ten simple lines as she had a million times before in her youth. The vacation that the poet wanted so desperately to remember. The lover who had detained him and made him lose track of everything else. They were together, so he forgot all the rest.

Chapter 22

Curse those three stupid dots. The typing awareness indicator had been all that Viola had been able to think about all morning.

After her conversation with Hannah, she'd gone home and sat on her couch for a very long time. She felt paralyzed. Stuck. *Too late.* Thanks a lot, writing background; Viola had entirely too many synonyms for "completely hopeless." She knew what she wanted, and she knew it more clearly than anything else: she wanted to be with Brooks. But he was in Charlotte with another woman. What could she really do about it?

Viola had started to type out a message, but it felt wrong. She had erased it immediately and then returned to pacing her tiny apartment living room. Duncan was beginning to lose his mind, dizzying himself as he followed Viola in circles, begging loudly for more cat treats.

Finally, Viola had decided to get smart. She opened up her laptop and started a new document. She poured her thoughts into a message, crafting exactly what she wanted to say to Brooks. When she felt ready, she typed it out carefully on her little iPhone screen.

She immediately hit delete once more.

She tried several other messages. They all felt right in the Word doc, but they failed as soon as she actually considered the ramifications of pressing send on her phone. For days, off and on, she wrote out new messages and erased them, distracting herself in between attempts by helping with Ruby's final wedding plans and refining the draft of her book that Francine had sent back to her.

And then the worst had happened. She'd been typing up a particularly lengthy message onto her iPhone when she saw three tiny dots appear in the left-hand corner of the screen. Brooks was messaging her, too! *But wait...* That meant that he could see her typing out this long message. The three stupid dots would surely be on his screen, as well. He'd see that she was typing first and typing something long, and he would almost definitely know that she was about to say something stupid or needy or embarrassing.

By the time that Viola had come to this conclusion, his three dots had disappeared. Brooks never messaged her anything. Clearly, he had seen through her crazy and decided not to reach out after all. Viola had somehow managed to make a worse impression for herself by not even saying a dang word.

On the morning of Ruby's wedding, she was still stuck on the three dots. Technology was going to kill her.

"Viola," Ruby breathed, bringing her back to reality. "You've really outdone yourself."

Her sister stepped through the doors of her dressing room and greeted the small crowd of bridesmaids. Ruby's gown was magnificent. It was a milky cream, fringed in fragile antique lace. The cape billowed behind her, making her look simultaneously powerful and delicate. Viola had woven her hair into a loose crown braid, letting Ruby's natural curls fall in soft ringlets around her heart-shaped face. With a soft blush on her cheeks and a warm pink on her lips, she was the definition of the perfect demure bride.

Viola was instantly brought back to the here and now. She was surprised to feel her breath catch in her throat and tears burn at the corners of her eyes. "Ruby, you're a *princess*."

"The music is going to start soon," Nadine warned everyone. "You finished up just in time."

Ruby took her sister's hand and stepped forward. "Somebody better lead the way to the chapel. I'm afraid that I was so nervous walking in here that I hardly paid any attention."

The girls formed a band and headed out down a bright hallway. Viola started to follow, when Ruby pulled her back.

Vi's sister tucked a loose strand of long black hair behind her ear and then ran a cautious thumb across her cheekbone. Ruby touched her as though Viola was something new and wondrous, a beautiful animal she had never come across before.

"You really made everything special, Vi," Ruby said. She hesitated then, clearly choosing her next words with care. The blush on her cheeks deepened. "I spoke with Nadine before the ceremony. I want you by my side as Maid of Honor. I want you back."

Viola could feel her eyes widen. "Roo, you don't have to—"

"I want to, silly." Ruby laughed and reached out to squeeze her sister's shoulder.

Before she was even aware of the emotion she felt, Viola started to cry. She could feel the tears running down her face in fat, wide drops. She tried to wipe them up, laughing as she did. "You've gone and ruined my make-up. Thanks a lot."

Ruby smiled. "I don't know what happened exactly, but something changed in you recently. You really came through for me."

At the mention of change, Viola's mind flashed away from Ruby once more to *him*. His dark head of curly hair. His teasing, flirtatious smile. She looked to the floor, busying herself with shuffling in her heels. She knew exactly what it was that had changed in her life.

"It's Brooks, isn't it?" The question came from Ruby as more of a statement. She knew that he had possessed Viola, that he had been all she could think about for weeks, and that preparing for the wedding had been a mere distraction.

"I don't know what to do," Viola confessed. "I had hoped that throwing myself into your wedding would distract me, but it didn't. I want to go after him. I want to run away and hide. I want to pretend that he never existed. For the first time in my life, I feel like love is real, and I might actually deserve it—but I have no idea what to do about it."

"That's why love is so worth it, you boob." Ruby nudged her with her foot. She took her by the small of her back and began to guide her down the hallway. "It's terrifying. But high risk means high reward. You have to go after him."

They could hear the music start and picked up the pace to find the other bridesmaids. Nadine spotted Viola and handed her a bouquet of marigolds and blush-colored roses. She gestured to her spot in line, and Ruby and Vi both fell into place.

Viola took deep breaths, forcing her tears to stay at bay as she regained her composure. Ruby gave her hand one last squeeze before her father stepped up to walk her down the aisle.

"I'm not going to get to really talk to you again until after your honeymoon," Viola moaned to her in a whisper. "How am I supposed to figure out what to do without you?"

"I think I might have an idea or two." Ruby winked.

Viola turned. It was her turn to walk down the aisle. She slipped her arm through that of a waiting groomsman and took her first steps forward.

The chapel transported her. Viola had been there late the night before, slaving away with Hannah and Nadine and the rest of the girls as she strung flowers and hung up decorative signs, but the darkness of the evening had masked the full effect. Now, as she took in the sight in front of a sea of expectant, beaming faces, she realized how incredible their work had truly been.

They'd brought local trees in and masses of flowers. They were draped from the walls and the ceiling, a thousand colors blooming all at once. They rained down on the bridesmaids and groomsmen, immersing them in a full forest. As she walked, Viola crushed soft apricot marigold petals underfoot, strewn by a flower girl wearing her own woven crown braid. At last, Viola found her spot at the front of the chapel. Her groomsman released her arm, and she stood, trying her best to keep holding it together.

The music shifted into something slow and dreamy. Ruby emerged from the chapel doors, and the guests all swooned. But Viola wasn't looking them; she was watching Scott for his reaction. Seemingly all at once, his face went through a thousand emotions. He was excited, that was clear by his broad, toothy grin. He was scared, too. Viola could see it in the deep blue wells of his eyes. But, more than anything else, it hit her how love-struck he was. Scott looked as though he couldn't stand to wait at the front of the chapel any longer. Like he wanted to run down the aisle and scoop up his bride and disappear into the forest of flowers they had arranged for their wedding.

The expression on his face looked like the most natural thing in the world.

Viola couldn't help it anymore. The tears were back, and they were coming full force. She ugly cried, with big gulps for air and mascara that pooled in sticky black circles under her eyes. Viola sent out a *thank you* to whatever God might reside in this chapel as the music swelled, and Ruby joined the group gathered round the pastor. Hopefully, no one could hear Vi's loud, rasping breaths over the Taylor Swift piano.

The pastor started in on the ceremony, and Viola finally managed to get it together. She found herself laughing at the lame wedding humor, feeling her heart warm with pride as Scott and Ruby exchanged their vows. It was the first wedding in a very long time that Viola didn't have a single cynical thought. She couldn't have written the day out better herself.

When the ceremony was over and Scott had planted a massive smooch on his giggling bride, Viola hollered louder than anyone else. She raised both fists in the air, cheering like she was at a UGA ballgame. Scott emerged from the kiss looking a little disheveled, smoothing his hair and glancing at the cheering Viola with a little bit of embarrassment and a little more pride.

They began the walk back down the aisle, with Scott and Ruby leading the way as a newly married couple. Viola followed, bursting at the seams as she crossed back through the chapel doors. She was surprised when she felt Ruby at her side, pulling her away from the group once more. The bouquet of chrysanthemums was being shoved into her hands, along with something small and metal.

"What's this?" She asked, puzzled.

"I told you that I had an idea or two up my sleeve," Ruby said with a smile. "So here's the plan. The bouquet is yours. I'm officially dubbing you the next woman here to find her love story, and I'm the bride so you're really not allowed to argue with me."

Viola fished out the metal item, holding it up to the light. "Are these your car keys?"

"You've got to get to Charlotte somehow." Ruby shrugged, looking mischievous. "Sorry if the car is decorated already. I didn't exactly give Scott's brothers the memo that I'd be sending you off like this."

Viola took a step back, feeling overwhelmed. "Ruby, I can't take your car. You've got your honeymoon to get to—"

Ruby waved her off. "We'll take Scott's car. Drove here separately anyway."

"But—"

Ruby put a finger to Viola's lips and grinned. "I know that you're the romance writer but let me have this one, will you? I want you to cash in on every part of the fairy tale."

Viola shook her head in disbelief. "I don't know what to say, Roo."

"Just go get 'em, tiger."

Ruby laughed as Scott ran up and swept her up off of her feet. He carried her away toward the reception hall, hooting and hollering like a teenaged party boy.

Viola looked down in her hands at the small set of car keys. Ruby had really outdone herself.

Chapter 23

Viola started the long, dark drive to Charlotte in Scott and Ruby's car, which had been decked to the nines in honeymoon decorations. She'd had to run it through a car wash twice before hitting the interstate, and two cans tied to the back were somehow still entangled, clanging, and brightly sparking on the road behind her. She frequently had to wave off strangers who looked at her a bit funny when they honked at her "Just Married" sign in the rear window only to see her riding alone, sans wedding dress.

It was comical how many of the feelings that Viola had once written about ironically she was now experiencing. Most obvious was her racing heart. She had thought she might be sick at first, but slowly she came to realize over the course of her drive that these were nerves. Her heart was pounding so hard that her chest ached.

Then there was the sweat. The drive from Atlanta to Charlotte took nearly four hours, but Viola couldn't help but feel worried that she'd still pull up to Brooks' place and look like she was dissolving. Despite blasting the A/C, her nerves had clearly gotten the best of her, and she could see in her rearview mirror that her makeup was melting down her face. Her hair had long since gone limp, sagging around her ears and neck in a tangled mess.

But what surprised Viola most of all was her energy. This was a feeling she knew well from writing it into nearly every book she had ever published. That inexplicable force, pulling two lovers together from wherever they were. She could feel it now, the tie to Brooks even though she hadn't spoken to him in forever and he was states away. She wanted time to speed up. She found herself flying down the interstate.

And before she knew it, she had made it to the city. Charlotte rose up around her in the dark of the night, its buildings lit up with sparkling lights and its trees standing tall and shadowed. Viola only had a vague idea of where she was going. Ruby had slipped her a scrap of paper with the bouquet, an address she had obtained from Aaron. Viola pulled it from her pocket now and grasped the paper in her palm to enter the numbers into her phone. She navigated the streets, feeling the beating in her chest growing stronger and stronger. She would almost swear that she could hear her heart out loud.

Finally, Viola found his street and turned in. She parked, looking up at the townhome Brooks shared with Emily Norman.

There was a light on in one of the windows. She could feel her blood freeze in her veins, paralyzing her. Someone was awake. Was it Brooks? Was it Emily? Oh gosh, what could she possibly say to Emily...

But what would she say to Brooks if it was him? All those hours spent driving and somehow the words still eluded Viola.

She pulled down her mirror and took a quick peek at

her reflection. She looked even worse than she thought. Mascara had pooled in deep wells under her eyes, and her red lipstick had cracked and faded, leaving her with a joker's smile. Her hair had almost entirely fallen from its updo, curling and frizzing around her neck and shoulders. Viola still wore her bridesmaid's dress, the creamsicle chiffon clinging to the areas of her skin where she had sweated the most. She was a mess. There was no nice way to say it. Certainly not how she had imagined looking when she confessed her feelings to Brooks.

But it would have to do. Viola swallowed down her pride and opened the car door. She forgot that she was wearing heels and stumbled a bit on the pavement. She could feel a shaking starting deep inside her as she took the steps up to his front door. *Control yourself. Calm down.* She reached forward to knock—

The door swung forward, knocking her off balance. Viola caught herself just in time on the stairwell.

"Reed?"

Brooks was standing in the doorway wearing a baseball cap and jacket, a bag slung over his shoulder. He reached out a hand to help Viola up. "What are you—"

"It's a lot to explain," Viola started. She could hardly catch her breath to get the words out.

They stood in silence for a moment, each taking the other in. Viola could feel the deep blush overtaking her cheeks as Brooks scanned over her crumpled bridesmaid dress and lackluster updo. A familiar smile pulled up at the corners of his mouth until he was grinning.

"Did you come from—"

"Where are you—"

They laughed at their old tendency to speak at the same time. Any discomfort dissipated. Viola smiled at him.

"You first," he said.

She shuffled a bit, avoiding his eyes. "I, uh, I just came from Ruby's wedding."

"Yeah, I can see that."

"She gave me your address."

Brooks' brow pinched in the middle, and he cocked his head. Viola shifted, trying to be brave as he examined her further. "And why did you need to come all the way out here?"

She shook her head. *Come on, Viola. You're a writer. Coming up with the right words is what you do for a living.*

"I missed you," she started. Saying the words out loud infused her with courage. She could feel a surge inside of her, propelling her forward to the rest of her confession. "And I don't want to be apart. Not anymore. I don't want to be your friend. And I don't want you to see other people. I certainly don't want you to live four hours away with a beautiful dental office manager."

"What *do* you want, Viola?" Brooks' hand slid along the railing nearer to hers. Viola could smell his cologne, that warm, inviting spiced scent that had clung to the jacket he left behind in her apartment. She could hardly breathe. "Say it."

She closed her eyes briefly. Said a quick prayer.

"I want you," she said. "I want you, Brooks. Be with me... because I love you."

Her racing heart seemed to stop as she held her breath. Brooks' eyes searched hers for a moment, puzzling her out. Finally, he stepped back, letting loose with a laugh. Viola's stomach flipped.

"Jeez, I really hate to disappoint you." He laughed.

Viola started to back down the stairs. "I'm so sorry," she said. "I shouldn't have come. You're happy here..."

"No, no," Brooks interrupted, reaching out his hand to take hers. "I just hate to make you give this big dramatic profession of love, and then I'm just going to go off and make it even more miserable and cliched for you."

"What?" She shook her head, trying to clear it.

Brooks slipped the bag off of his shoulder and held it up. "I was on my way to catch a flight," he said. "Charlotte to Atlanta. Red eye. I was coming to see you."

"You were... coming to see me." She repeated. The words didn't sound real.

"I broke things off with Emily a few days ago. Turns out there was someone else that I couldn't stop thinking about."

"You were coming to see me," Viola repeated, her voice a whisper. She started to smile.

"I was coming to see you," Brooks said again, laughing.

He pulled Viola up the stairs and pressed her to his chest. She pulled off his baseball cap and tossed it behind them. She ran her fingers through his thick, dark curls, adoring the way they felt on her fingers. She'd wanted to do this for so long, and now she could do this any time she wished, *because he was hers.* He put a hand to the nape of her neck, his fingers light to the touch on the flushed skin.

"You were coming to see me." Viola sang the words, teasing Brooks. "*You* were coming to see *me*."

"I was coming to see you." He grinned before pulling her to him.

Brooks kissed her then, the kind of kiss that can't be described with ink and paper. It transcended romance novels, tropes, canned plots. Viola had experienced nothing like it before. She held him close, never wanting the moment to end.

He pulled back suddenly, water splashing them from seemingly out of nowhere. "Jeez!"

Brooks scrambled away from her, dashing onto the little townhome lawn where the sprinklers had started going off. One sprinkler head was going berserk, spraying water in every direction, and entirely soaking where they had stood together on the stairs.

Brooks approached the sprinkler, warding off water with one hand as he fidgeted with the other. Finally, the sprinkler relented to spray its wild deluge against the window rather than onto the new lovers. Brooks looked up at Viola. His clothes were thoroughly soaked through, and his face was sour and annoyed.

"Been meaning to fix that sprinkler since I got here," he grumbled. He shook out his wet hair before pulling his shirt up and over his head. He discarded it on the railing. "I'd better change real quick."

Viola started giggling. The laugh bubbled up inside of her until it overtook her completely. She was full-on snorting, bending over to grasp onto the railing as she laughed and laughed.

"What?" Brooks asked, laughing, too, and stepping up to be beside her once more. "Did I just blow it?"

"No, no way." Viola struggled to regain her composure. She stood up, wiping away tears from the corners of her eyes. "It's just... I think you're my Jean-Luc."

"What?"

"I spent forever trying to figure out how my stupid male lead was going to take his shirt off. I tried a rainstorm. A cup of water spilling on him. He's got to look sexy for his big moment with the heroine, right?"

Brooks shrugged and smiled, adorably confused. "Okay?"

"And here you are. We kiss, the sprinklers turn on, and

suddenly you're shirtless and ready to kiss me." Viola started laughing again. She doubled over. "You're Jean-Luc!"

"It only gets more cheesy from here," Brooks said with a laugh of his own. He stepped toward her, pulling her close once more.

"I could not care less." She kissed him deeply, still thoroughly amused as the sprinklers rained on.

CHAPTER 24

AUTUMN

"Ugh, I really hate weddings."

"Don't be such a sourpuss, Reed." Brooks elbowed Viola and offered her some sparkling punch he had snagged from the bar.

She took it, grateful, and downed it in one big gulp. Brooks took back the empty glass, smiling at her.

He looked good, very much like the first night they met. He wore a slick, tailored black suit with a little green bow tie. He had a pocket square, too, a frivolous detail that Viola had mocked him for when they found it at J. Crew, but she had to admit that it looked pretty darn dashing when he wore it now. He had the miniature tiger cufflinks on his arms. He wore the spicy cologne that she liked so much. Not too shabby at all.

He settled back in his chair, folding his arms. He pointed at a couple canoodling at a table nearby. "Okay, let's have some fun here." He held up his hands to frame the couple like a picture. "I'm placing my bets on the coat closet at reception. Definitely."

"No way," Viola shook her head. "He's already touching

her knee, and she's *twirling his tie*. Read the signs, Hardison. He'll make his move right here."

"Come on; that's tacky even by *my* standards." Brooks dismissed her, still smiling. "Everyone gets together at weddings, but no one is drunk enough to make out right at the table."

They watched as the boy whispered something in the girl's ear. She giggled, her cheeks turning bright red before she reached over and grabbed him to kiss him.

"Oh!" Brooks and Viola laughed in unison as they caught a glimpse of tongue.

"Who invited these people?" Brooks asked.

"Who are we to complain?" Viola teased as she flagged down a waiter. He offered up a platter of food, and she selected her appetizers with care. "We get dinner and a show! Now pay up, Hardison. Go ahead and admit that I know more about this stuff than you do."

Hannah and Aaron approached their table. Hannah was in the full swing of her third trimester, her belly round and heavy, bouncing as she walked. She pulled out a chair at their table and sat down.

"Okay," she said, wincing. "That last dance was definitely a mistake."

Aaron laughed and sat down at the table adjacent to them. "I don't know, darlin'; I think the whole reception appreciated the show."

She smiled and shot him a look before turning to Vi and Brooks. "You two have to get out there soon, you know."

"I've been telling her all night." Brooks threw up his hands, innocent.

"You can convince me to wear these three-inch heels, but you absolutely cannot convince me to dance in them,"

Viola told Hannah. "People will be talking about the debacle I'll make for ages."

"Trust me; no one will be talking about anythin' except for the pregnant chick who got down to 'Baby Got Back.'" Aaron grinned and Hannah heaved herself up to slap him on the arm.

"Did you forget to invite us?"

The group turned to see Ruby and Scott heading their way. They sat down next to Aaron at the nearby table.

"Vi, you're going to dance soon, right?" Ruby asked.

"See?" Brooks nudged her. "Your public demands it."

"My public can shove off," Viola said. She held up her plate of food. "Besides, I just got my eggrolls. I'm happy!"

A text sounded and Aaron looked down at his phone. He laughed before realizing the group was watching, then he pocketed the device. He looked pretty sheepish.

"And who, pray tell, is important enough to interrupt our night together?" Brooks mocked him. "I don't wanna be *that guy*, but we've kind of had this wedding on the books for ages."

Aaron winced. "... It's Matt."

Hannah elbowed him. "He forced my hand!" Aaron said, throwing his hands in the air.

"Matt insists on maintaining a friendship," Hannah apologized for her husband. "If I didn't have to waddle to get after my husband, I'd do somethin' about it."

Viola waved them off though, smiling. "It's okay. Actually... we kind of set him up, so we're not on bad terms."

"You set up your ex?" Ruby repeated.

"With Brooks' ex." She laughed out loud as they all went wide-eyed with surprise. "We thought they might get along. I mean, she was pretty, he was pretty. It seemed like a match made in heaven. But, it was—"

"A complete disaster," Aaron jumped in. "He just texted me that he's never been out with someone before who uses the phrase 'for the Gram' seriously."

They all laughed, and Aaron held up the little phone screen to show them the messages. "But actually, guys, I kind of think you might have done Matt a favor. He just messaged me that he's got some tour to Africa all booked. He's gonna eat, pray, love it 'til the cows come home."

The music faded, and the lights dimmed. A spotlight searched the floor as the wedding planner got up on the stage, gesturing for the guests to simmer down.

"Alright, everyone, it's that time! It's my pleasure to present to you for the first time as a married couple, Mr. and Mrs. Brooks Hardison!"

The spotlight swung over to their table, where Viola had an egg roll halfway in her mouth. She eyeballed Brooks, who suppressed a smile. "You may not have a choice anymore," he murmured to her.

Viola begrudgingly set down the egg roll and stood up, waving at her guests. Brooks offered her his hand and led her away from the table, out onto the dance floor. The music picked up, shifting into big, brassy swing music.

Viola's eyes lit up as she got into position. "You did not! I put a very specific 'No Chance to Embarrass Viola' clause into our wedding plan. I might be a good swing dancer, but even I can't come back from my wedding guests getting a full view of my underwear as you swing me over your head."

"Hey, it's our night. If we have to suffer through this, then we might as well get to do the things we like to do." Brooks smiled and pulled her close.

The beat set off and so did the couple. Brooks twirled her around, spinning her until she was laughing and dizzy.

When he picked her up and threw her into the air, her heels flew off. The crowd cheered.

Finally, the swing music faded and shifted into their more traditional first dance music. Someone came over and returned her heels to her. After laughingly putting them back on, Viola smiled as Brooks pulled her close, and she set her head on his shoulder. Even though she had danced to Ed Sheeran's "Thinking Out Loud" at a million weddings before her own, she couldn't help but feel happy as they swayed to the tune together.

Viola felt a tap on her shoulder, and she stopped and turned.

"I think it might be time for me to cut in." Her father stood with his hand outstretched. Brooks nodded at him and passed over Viola.

Dan Reed looked the closest to emotional that Viola had ever seen him. He held his daughter close and pulled her head down to his chest.

"You picked a good one, kiddo," he said. "You got real lucky."

"No." Viola lifted her head and shook it. "I finally got smart."

She could see her father's eyes cut across the dance floor, where his date was waiting for him to return. His time with Wife Number Four had burned bright and fast, and he had been single and dating again before Brooks had even put a ring on it.

For the first time, Viola thought that her father looked sad. His eyes were hollow and empty, and it occurred to her that he might not just be congratulating her on her big day. He might be jealous.

"How did you pull that off?" He asked Viola, looking at her seriously.

"You'll figure it out, Dad," she said, pulling him close again and nestling in on his shoulder. "If Duncan and I can find our Mr. Right, then you can find your soul mate, too."

Her father laughed. "You did get lucky that you found a man who is willing to let your cat still sleep in your bed with you."

"Don't forget eat at the kitchen table."

"And watch Animal Planet all day when you're gone on long trips."

Viola pulled back, and they grinned at each other. She squeezed her dad's shoulders as the music started to fade out. "Real love will happen for you," she assured him. "You just can't be afraid to go find it."

She felt Brooks come up to her side, offering his hand to lead her back to their table.

"You all good?" He asked as they walked. "Things looked kind of serious back there."

"We're all good," she affirmed, nodding.

"So," Viola briskly changed the subject, her eyes twinkling with mischief as she glanced back over at her new husband. "Do you think the bridesmaids will freak if I forego the bouquet tossing and keep the flowers for myself? They're too pretty to give up."

Brooks slapped a hand to his forehead in feigned dramatics. "Reed, you're killing me! All brides toss the bouquet. The only reason they don't is if they're selfish, they've had a medical emergency, or they're busy hooking up with their new spouse in a coat closet. Basic Wedding 101. Where is your superpower these days?"

"So if I hook up with my new spouse in the coat closet, does that mean that I can keep the flowers?"

After playfully thinking for a moment, Brooks winked at her. "I'll allow it."

"Okay," Viola grinned as they slipped out of the reception hall together. "But you're going to have to compliment me on my *Star Wars* themed garter when you find it."

"*Star Wars*? Are you kidding me?"

And with that, the couple snuck out of their own wedding reception, holding hands and giggling. Viola couldn't have written their ending any better herself.

REVIEW

We hope you've enjoyed Completely Undatable.

If you did, please consider leaving a review on Amazon or Goodreads. Reviews can do so much for up and coming authors and your thoughts would be appreciated.

ABOUT THE AUTHOR

Brittni is up and coming in published fiction, but oh-so-familiar to the pen. An accomplished comedian, writer, and performer, she has delighted audiences for years all over the country.

Now she's bringing her wit and attitude to the printed page with heartfelt, sweet, and raw contemporary romance.

Connect on Facebook to hear the latest about her upcoming books!

ALSO BY BRITTNI MINER

Call it Kismet

From the Top

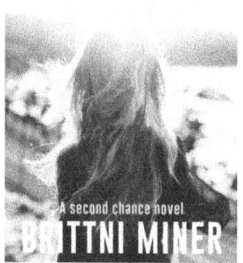